D1784041

FATHER

OF THE

Groom

Silvia Violet

Father of the Groom by Silvia Violet

Copyright © 2018 by Silvia Violet

Cover art by Jay Aheer

Edited by Courtney Bassett

All Rights Reserved. No part of this eBook may be used or reproduced in any manner whatsoever without written permission except in brief quotations embodied in critical articles or reviews.

Published in the United States of America.

Father of the Groom is a work of fiction. Names, places, characters, and incidents are either the product of the author's imagination or are fictionalized. Any resemblance to any actual persons, living or dead, is entirely coincidental.

CHAPTER ONE

AVERY

I rushed down a hallway in the Misty Mountain Lodge, trying not to let myself get distracted by the eclectic mix of paintings—modern art, Victorian ladies taking a stroll, something vaguely cubist—or the delicious smells coming from someone's room service cart. I was already late, and Felicity was going to murder me if her makeup wasn't perfect for her big day. I'd meant to leave work earlier than I had, but the salon was always crazy on Fridays, so now I was running late.

I still couldn't believe Felicity was actually getting married today. In just a few hours, actually. I felt like we'd been planning and stressing—and laughing at how much we were stressing—about this wedding forever.

I had to be close to her room; I was almost at the end of the corridor. Three sixteen. Three eighteen. There it was. Three twenty. Of course it would be on the corner. She and Carter had reserved an enormous suite since they were spending their wedding night here before heading to a resort in Trinidad. I wasn't sure they'd really make use of the space, though, not like I would. Carter seemed so vanilla. Though for all I knew he was hiding some dark secrets behind that khakis-and-polo facade. Whatever they did in bed, Felicity loved him. I was sure of that. Not that I'd ever admit it to her, but I was all kinds of jealous. I could get all the sex I wanted—kinky or otherwise—as long as I put a little effort into it, but love was something that had eluded me.

I knocked on the door and Christy, Felicity's roommate, yanked it open a few seconds later.

"Avery, you're finally here!" Felicity shrieked. Christy grabbed my arm, and I basically fell into the room.

"I'm not that late," I huffed.

"Not by your standards, but there are three of us who need makeup, and I know you like to take your time and—"

"Shhh." I kissed her cheek. "It's all going to be fine."

Brandy, a friend who worked at the Oasis Asheville with me, had already fixed Felicity's and her bridesmaid's hair. She was the queen of updos, and while I still loved styling hair, I was focused more on makeovers these days.

"Have you seen Carter?" Felicity asked as I opened my bag and started taking out my supplies.

"No, haven't you?"

"No!" Her volume was back to the screech she'd used when I'd first arrived. "A bride doesn't see her groom on their wedding day. What are you thinking?"

"You told me, and I quote, 'I don't go in for all that superstitious wedding bullshit.'"

"So I changed my mind, what of it?"

Yikes. She had her scary face on; no way was I going to argue. "Nothing. Nothing at all. Change your mind whenever you like."

"Fuck right I will."

Christy's phone chimed and she picked it up. "Wren says their dad's finally here. He was stuck in traffic driving up from Charlotte."

Felicity sighed. "I really hope this goes all right."

Wren was Carter's younger brother. Their dad had come out as gay seven or eight years ago. The divorce was ugly, and Carter's mom still didn't speak to him. She'd done everything she could to prevent Carter's dad from seeing him, Wren, or their sister, Mandy. Carter had been estranged from his dad for years, but they'd repaired their relationship a few years ago, when Mandy came out as a lesbian and their mom reacted badly. Things with Carter's mom were still strained, and the whole situation was rather volatile.

"How worried should we be?" I asked.

Felicity was busy fiddling with a pin that had slipped out of her hair, but Hillary, her other bridesmaid, answered. "Mandy stopped by earlier and said her mom was in a better mood since their dad skipped the rehearsal dinner, but Carter is about to lose his mind over whether they can keep it together through the whole ceremony."

"Mandy was here?"

"Yep. You just missed her."

"Dammit. Is she dressed already? I wanted to see her in her tux." Mandy was Carter's best woman, and when I'd found out she was going to dress like the rest of the groomsman, I'd considered wearing a bridesmaid dress for my role, which Felicity liked calling Twink of Honor, but since I wasn't used to walking in heels, I decided not to risk falling on my way down the aisle.

"So Carter's parents still haven't spoken?" I asked.

"No," Felicity said. "And if you see them on a collision course, please do anything you can to stop it."

"Anything?" I raised a brow.

"Okay, maybe that was too far."

"It won't be easy for me anyway, since I don't know what his dad looks like."

"He's way hot," Christy said.

Hillary nodded vigorously. "He totally is."

I looked to Felicity for confirmation. "Fine. They're right."

We were going to talk later about why she'd never mentioned this. "Okay then. How's your mom? Is she here?"

Felicity's mom, unlike Carter's, was awesome. She'd never had any problem with me being exactly who I was. She'd raised Felicity on her own, and I knew she was as proud of the woman Felicity had grown into as I was.

"She's great. She's picking up Grandma and then she'll be here."

"Great. Should we get started?"

Felicity didn't answer. Instead, she narrowed her eyes at me, studying me intently.

"What?"

"Did you have to make yourself look so good I can't measure up?"

"I have no idea what you mean," I said, summoning my best humble tone.

"You know you look amazing."

I did. I'd started using an eyelash lengthening serum that worked like magic. My now-lush lashes looked amazing with the soft pink color I'd put on my lids. The brighter pink lip stain I'd chosen set off the look to make me extremely kissable. There wasn't anyone at the wedding I planned to kiss, but I had every intention of finding someone at my favorite club once the reception wound down. Actually, that someone better do a hell of a lot more than kiss me.

"I look fabulous, but you will look even better, as is the bride's prerogative." I gestured toward the sofa. "Have a seat and let me find what I need."

"All right. But do Christy and Hillary first; I'm too nervous to sit."

I squeezed her hand. "This evening is going to be perfect."

"You really think so?"

"I do. And Carter loves you so much. I see it every time he looks at you."

Christy made gagging sounds, and I glared at her. "Do not interrupt me trying to cheer up the bride."

"Enough cheering, more makeup sorcery," Felicity demanded.

"Hmmm. Sorceress of Honor has a nice ring to it."

Felicity shook her head. "Twink of Honor suits you much better."

"No, I've got it. Queen of Honor. That's it. That's my title, or you can stand up there by yourself."

Felicity glanced over at her roommate. "Christy, I've got a new job for you."

I gave her a look of mock outrage. "Is that really how you want to talk to your makeup *queen* when he's about to make you beautiful?"

She fixed me with her Scary Bride Stare.

"Fine. I relent, just calm down and let me work."

By the time I'd finished with the makeovers for all three of them, I wished I'd done my own makeup last. I hadn't realized how sweaty I'd get trying to keep Felicity calm and make everyone look perfect. At least I wasn't dressed yet, so I could do a little refresh wash of the most pertinent areas.

"Did you bring your tux?" Felicity asked when I stepped out from the bathroom.

"Of course. Did you think I was going to get dressed with the boys?"

She huffed. "Obviously not."

Next came a flurry of crinolines and hot pink retro dresses. Hillary was admiring herself in the bathroom mirror, so I slipped into the walk-in closet to change pants, since I planned to wear a jock strap instead of my briefs. No way was I going to risk lines marring the perfection of my tight tuxedo pants. The cut was the same as the groomsmen, but I had a hot pink vest and a pink polka dot bowtie as opposed to the classic black they'd be wearing.

Once I was fully dressed, Felicity fussed with my tie and tugged on the vest, saying it needed straightening. I let her "help" since I could tell she needed something to do. When she finished, I took her hands in mine. "Are you okay?"

She frowned. "I think so. Maybe."

"You know Carter's the one who ought to be nervous."

"Yeah?"

"Sure. He's going to have to put up with you for like decades."

She shoved me away and held up her middle finger.

"You know he's right," Christy said.

9

"Fine," she huffed. "I'm a lot to take sometimes."

"That's for damn sure," Hillary said.

"At least you don't live with her," Christy said. Then she frowned. "I guess I don't anymore, though."

That statement made Felicity go all mushy, and I could see the threat of tears. "Don't you dare cry. Not after all the work I've done."

"It's my wedding. Of course I'm going to cry. I already told you that. This stuff had better be waterproof." She gestured toward her eyes.

"It is, but you can still smudge it. Can't you at least hold off until you actually walk down the aisle?"

"Maybe."

"How long before we need to be in our places?" Christy asked.

I glanced at my phone. "Thirty minutes."

"Hmpf, that didn't take as long as I expected," Felicity said. "Avery, will you do me a favor?"

"Of course, my love, what do you need?"

"Go check on Carter."

"We could just text Mandy or Wren."

Felicity shook her head. "You'll be able to tell how he's doing a lot better in person, and once you've checked in on him, I need you to make sure everything is running smoothly with the caterers."

I resisted the urge to remind her that she had a very expensive wedding planner whose job it was to do that. I also didn't whine about how I'd rather stay with her and gossip, because that's the kind of friend I was. "I'll let you know once I've talked to Carter, okay?"

"Thank you."

"Of course. Anything for you, especially today." I would take care of her today, give her whatever she needed, like she'd done for me so many times over the years. I knew how good it felt to know there was someone you could count on to make sure things went just right for you. She had Carter now, though. And I would see her a lot less often. If only I had someone else to swoop in to make things right for me. Not that I wasn't perfectly independent. I could take care of myself. It was just a drag to always have to.

CHAPTER TWO

GRAHAM

I watched my son walking toward me across the vast hotel ballroom and smiled. There'd been a time a few years ago when I'd thought I would miss out on this and all other important moments in his life. I was so thankful that he and Mandy had come to me when their mom refused to accept that Mandy was gay. My ex had the nerve to ask Mandy if she'd been talking to me, insinuating that I'd converted her to the gay agenda. But thanks to Louise poisoning her against me, I hadn't talked to Mandy in years at that point.

"Thank you for being here," Carter said.

I pulled him into a hug. "I love you, Carter, and I would never—not even when you stopped speaking to me—turn down a chance to be at your wedding."

"I love you too, Dad."

When he pulled back, Carter wiped at his eyes and looked away for a moment, which was fine with me. I needed to compose myself too. This was going to be an emotional whirlwind of a day.

A few seconds later, Carter said, "Mom's here. She's with Jennifer and Ron, her favorite homophobic friends."

Yep. I was definitely going to hit all the emotional highs and lows today. "Why are they here?"

Carter raised his brows, and I sighed because I knew, even though I hated that they got to share in this day. "They've known you since you were in preschool, and it wasn't worth the argument?"

He nodded. "Listen, just… just don't try to talk to them, okay?"

I tensed. Did he really think I would? "I'm not going to start trouble at your wedding. I don't want any trouble with your mother. I never did." I thought for a second about how that sounded. "I guess you think that's bullshit."

Carter shook his head. "You made mistakes, sure, but coming out to her was better than continuing to pretend. You were trying to correct a mistake."

"A huge one, one I'm still really sorry for, with one—no, three—exceptions."

Carter looked confused.

"You."

"Oh."

"And Mandy and Wren. I wouldn't have the three of you if I'd been honest all along, not that I really knew I was gay when you were born. I was so deep in denial I wouldn't have dared to admit it even to myself. I really thought… Well, that doesn't matter. All that matters today is that I'm here to support you. This should be a perfect day for you, and the last thing I want is for the unresolved shit between your mom and me to mess that up."

"It's not. I mean, I know you'll do everything you can to prevent that from happening."

I didn't want to say this, but I had to. "If it would be better for me to—"

"No. You already missed last night." His mother had insisted on hosting the rehearsal dinner, and we'd decided it was best if I didn't attend. "And… You missed so many other things. You will be here for this. It's what I want. What Mom wants doesn't matter, not today."

"You're right. I don't want to miss anything else. I want to be here, supporting you."

Carter nodded, but I could tell something was still bothering him.

"What's wrong?"

He shifted from one foot to the other. "I'm just really nervous."

"Felicity is an amazing woman."

"I know she is, but I just can't believe she actually wants to marry me."

"I can."

Carter scrunched up his nose. "Ugh. You're my dad. Of course you can."

Those words had tears pricking the backs of my eyes, because there'd been a time when I was sure Carter thought I didn't care about him at all. And now he not only wanted me here, he trusted me to help him through his jitters.

"Felicity adores you. I can see that every time you're together."

"Really?"

"Yes, really. I can give examples, if that would help."

Carter shook his head. "I don't think so. I… I think I'd rather talk about something else. Anything else. Just thinking about watching her walk down the aisle makes me feel like I'm going to pass out."

I smiled at him and patted his arm. "You're going to be fine. Why don't you tell me again about the rest of the wedding party? I want to be sure I've got everyone's names straight."

"Okay. I can do that. Obviously, you know Mandy and Wren."

I grinned. "Yeah, I do." Mandy and I were now closer than we'd ever been. Wren had only been thirteen when I'd left, and we were still trying to figure each other out, but we were getting there.

"And you said you remember Hal."

I nodded. He'd been one of Carter's best friends in high school. He'd been at our house most weekends, but I hadn't seen him in years.

"So then there's Christy, Felicity's roommate, and Hillary, one of her friends from college."

"And… Avery, right?"

"Yes, Avery…" Carter blushed a bit. "Her Twink of Honor is what she calls him."

I couldn't help but laugh. "He sounds very interesting."

"Yeah, like I told you, he's been her best friend since elementary school."

"And he's a makeup artist?"

"Right. He does hair too, but makeup is like his thing. He's really talented."

I was far more intrigued by Avery than I should be, considering he was my about-to-be daughter-in-law's best friend.

"He's also, um… a bit much. He wears makeup most of the time, and he considered wearing a bridesmaid dress. It took me a little while to get used to him, but we're good friends now too."

I wasn't going to tell Carter that I'd hooked up with plenty of femmes, so I just said, "What does your mother say about him?"

15

Carter rolled his eyes. "Nothing good, but I've made it very clear that she'd best keep quiet about that today."

I clenched my fists, anger burning through me. "If I even think she's going to say anything, I'll put a stop to it."

"Okay, but—"

"Just trust me."

I thought Carter was going to protest again, but instead he smiled. "Thanks. I better get back to the other guys now and finish getting ready."

"You want me to come along?"

He frowned. "I think Mom's coming by soon. She was bringing the boutonnières."

I tried not to let my disappointment show. "Okay, well, go on then."

"I'm sorry."

"Don't worry about it. We'll have lunch tomorrow. You'll be more relaxed to talk then anyway."

"Right. Lunch. Okay. I'll see you in a little while."

He turned and scurried off. I knew I should be grateful that he and Felicity wanted to hang out with me on what really should be the first day of their honeymoon, but it didn't stop me from being pissed as hell at my ex.

And I was going to have to circulate alone at the reception as I ran into people from my former life. Why hadn't I brought a plus one? I'd considered it, but the problem was, I really only did hookups and many of those were with guys Carter's age, so asking them to the wedding would be awkward at best. My best friend, Leo, would've come, and we did hook up occasionally, but I craved men who wanted to surrender, to let me be in charge, and Leo was even more dominant than I was. Oh well, maybe I'd go out after the reception. I sure as hell was going to need to release some tension after spending the evening avoiding my ex-wife and God only knew how many of my ex-friends.

CHAPTER THREE

AVERY

Carter assured me he was fine, and honestly, he didn't seem any closer to freaking out than Felicity was. It would be weird if he wasn't nervous at all, right? So I wished him and all the groomsmen luck—then second-guessed if that was the right thing to say. Were weddings a luck thing? Did you say break a leg or something weird like before a play? Oh well, no one had questioned it, and Carter probably wasn't really listening anyway.

Once I left the meeting room where they were dressing, I wove my way through the labyrinth of hotel corridors to the ballroom where the caterers were setting up the tables and buffet.

Everything appeared to be going well there. The tables were covered with white linens, and several men and women were placing vases of flowers as centerpieces. Chafing dishes lined the buffet ready to receive the various hot foods. I glanced around and saw Susan, the wedding coordinator. She waved and I walked over to her. "Is everything going all right?"

"Yes, we're right on schedule. Did Felicity send you?"

I nodded.

"Tell her not to worry. I've got this."

"Thanks."

I texted Felicity, and when I looked up from my phone, I saw what was probably the hottest silver fox I'd ever seen standing by the French doors that led into the gardens. Had he been there when I'd come in? If so, how the hell had I missed such an appetizing sight?

I started toward him, not even conscious of taking steps. Hot daddies like him were my magnetic north. He was wearing a tux that fit like it was tailored for him. Even with the jacket on, I could tell his ass was a work of art. I wanted to fall to my knees and worship it.

Shit. Now my cock was responding to that thought, and I really didn't want to meet Daddy Perfect Ass with an obvious boner.

He turned toward me then. Had he seen me watching him through the glass or just felt me staring? I looked him up and down, not even trying to hide the lust he inspired. Why should Felicity be the only one having fun tonight?

"Like what you see?" he asked.

"Maybe."

He looked pointedly at my crotch. "Oh, I think you do."

I couldn't protest his ungentlemanly behavior, because his dark-eyed stare and commanding tone rendered me incapable of speech. As did his obvious interest. He didn't even pretend to look away as I took a few steps closer.

An arrogant, dominant, older man. Oh hell, yeah, he was everything I wanted.

He slipped his jacket off and rolled his shoulders. Holy hell, this was like flirting times ten, a full-on display of his prowess. And his shirt looked like it might not survive the strain his chest was putting on it.

"Oh, Daddy." The words slipped out, and I should have regretted them, but I saw his eyes widen briefly before he controlled his expression again.

I was about to say something else, probably something ill-advised, when Carter came running in. "Dad, thank goodness you're still here."

Oh, fuck. *This* was Carter's dad. Wow. Hot didn't even begin to describe him. The tux should've been a signal that he was part of the wedding party, but I hadn't exactly been thinking clearly as I'd approached him. Heat rushed to my face, making me curse my pale skin. I prayed Carter wouldn't ask what was wrong. Maybe he was too distracted to notice that I'd been hitting on his fucking father.

I took a few steps back. "I'll let you two talk about whatever Carter needs. I-I'm sure you're busy, but it was nice to meet you, sir, and—"

"You didn't tell me your name," Mr. Hillingdon said.

Name. My name. What was it again? "Avery. I'm Avery."

"I suspected as much, and it's nice to meet you too." He held out his hand for me to shake, and I saw a mischievous glint in his eyes. The bastard was still flirting, even with Carter right there. And what did he mean he suspected it? He knew I was Carter's friend before he'd blatantly shown off for me?

I took his hand and damn, it was warm and big. He squeezed me just right, enough to show dominance but without crushing my fingers.

"Um. Nice to meet you too." There, I could remember basic social niceties.

"I hope to see you again later, Avery."

"Yeah. Yes. Me too. I'll… I'll see you later."

I backed away and then practically ran out of there.

Carter had to be wondering what the hell was wrong with me. Had I acted strangely enough that he'd text Felicity about it? I hoped not. If so, I'd just say I was getting more nervous as it got closer to time to line up for the ceremony.

The real question was, what would I do if/when I saw Carter's dad again?

Lay down and spread my legs?

No. Definitely not that.

I'd avoid him. That's what I'd do. Unless he was approaching Carter's mom, because I'd promised Felicity I'd make sure that didn't happen. Damn it. I'd just have to hope they had the sense to avoid a confrontation, because if I spent much time around that man I would be in big trouble. He was everything I couldn't resist.

CHAPTER FOUR

GRAHAM

I wandered through the reception accepting congratulations and doing my best to avoid any scenes with Louise or the friends of ours who'd sided with her and still refused to speak to me. I didn't really think she'd start anything. Surely, she wanted Carter's wedding to be perfect as much as I did, but there were a few of her friends who might not be able to keep their mouths shut, especially after a few glasses of champagne.

Once the dancing started, I danced with Mandy and then with Felicity. I spent some time talking to Wren and the other members of the wedding party, but after a tense moment when Louise came up to Hillary as I was introducing myself, I decided I needed some air.

I'd yet to talk to Avery again. I'd seen him in the ceremony, of course, and on the dance floor, but since then each time I'd noticed him, he'd been across the room or busy talking to someone I didn't know. I'd stared at him openly every time he'd caught my eye. He was so damn alluring I couldn't help myself. His dirty blond hair was cut close, except for the top which was smooth and slicked down. The bright pink of his vest and bow tie would have looked absurd on a lot of men, but they fit him perfectly. But what really held my attention were his lips, which were painted a slightly lighter shade of pink. Damn if I didn't want them wrapped around my cock while he looked up at me with those long-lashed hazel eyes that seemed to see right into me. He'd known what I wanted, not that I'd tried hard to hide it. If Carter hadn't come running in, I might have… What? Dragged him off somewhere private to have my wicked way with him? I was at my son's wedding. Surely I wasn't that big of a slut.

I wanted to go searching for him. But did I dare? He was my new daughter-in-law's best friend. Starting something with him was a terrible idea, even something that was just for tonight. My cock wasn't interested in logic, though, and I'd been walking around half-hard since I'd seen him gracefully dancing with a man I recognized as a work colleague of Carter's. Was there something between them? Jealousy flared at the thought, which was ridiculous. I needed to stay away from Avery.

Oh, Daddy. I couldn't get those words out of my head. As soon as he'd said it I'd wanted to put him on his knees. Would he play that game with me? Would he be a good boy? He'd look incredible stretched out on the enormous bed in my suite. He'd wanted me too, I was sure of it, but Carter and I were finally in a really good place. I should not risk screwing that up.

Carter won't know if it's just for one night.

That voice in my head was far too seductive. I could take Avery up to my room, fuck him until neither of us could move, and then let him go.

I wasn't sure the feelings Avery inspired were that simple, though. And that, even more than the fear of Carter finding out, was what held me back. The way Avery had looked at me, that pretend innocence, like he needed me to discipline him, needed someone to restrain him, literally and figuratively. I'd played enough at Leo's club to have developed an instinct for when a man craved submission. If I had to guess, I'd say Avery would love for me to take him in hand. And I wanted that. I wanted him to be my boy, so I could take care of him, which was crazy. I hardly knew him, and yet I longed to make sure he was safe, to teach him how to be good. But if we were going to do anything at all, it needed to be a fast hookup, one that ended after we both came.

I sighed as I made my way toward the doors that led onto the terrace. I'd take a walk, then come back and bid everyone good night. After that I'd either go to bed or seek some stress relief elsewhere.

Whether it was tonight or not, I seriously needed to get laid soon. It had been way too long, which was probably the explanation for my intense reaction to Avery. I could've sought someone out well before now. I just… hadn't really wanted to. When had it started to seem like too much trouble to use an app or go to a club? I wasn't sure. All I knew was that lately that seemed so… clinical? Heartless? Boring?

Since my divorce, I'd dismissed the importance of romance, but lately I wanted more than an anonymous hole to shove my dick in. I had a hand that worked just fine and a collection of sex toys. I could get myself off if that was all I needed.

A waiter passed by with a tray of champagne. I set my empty glass on it but didn't take another. I needed a real drink. I headed to the bar near the terrace doors. The beautiful young man behind it gave me an assessing look as I approached. I appreciated what that look offered, even if I didn't feel his gaze like fingers running down my body the way I had with Avery. If I took this man upstairs later, we could have a fun, uncomplicated evening.

"Can I help you, sir?" he asked, voice breathy.

"Oh, I think you can."

"Then I'm at your service."

Ask him.

I didn't. All I said was, "Scotch on the rocks."

"Yes, sir." I saw a flash of disappointment in his eyes, but he made the drink efficiently and handed it to me.

"Do come back if you need *anything* else."

The invitation couldn't have been more clear, and I should have taken him up on it. I was horny. I had a luxurious suite. But all I wanted was Avery. "Thank you. I'll remember that."

I passed by Wren as I headed outside. He was talking to a man who looked about his age. They were standing close. Wren's face was flushed, his smile wider than I was used to seeing it. The man said something, and Wren laughed and touched his arm. That was interesting. I slipped out before he noticed me watching him. I'd have to find a discreet way to ask Mandy what was up. She was far more likely to know Wren's secrets than Carter.

I took a deep breath when I stepped outside. The night was cool enough to be a relief from the hot afternoon and perfect for an evening stroll. I wandered down the terrace steps and into the gardens that ran along the back of the hotel. They were filled with an array of roses in every color. I sipped my drink as I read the names of the different varieties. I'd been meaning to do more with my yard; maybe I should try my hand at roses.

A few moments later, I heard footsteps behind me. At first, I figured it was someone else needing air or a couple who wanted some privacy. But when the person followed me as I turned down a narrow path, I turned around and saw Avery.

He froze and looked down, chewing his lip.

"You came after me."

"I…" He glanced up briefly, then lowered his eyes again.

I stepped closer so he could hear me whisper. "Don't argue with me, boy."

His gasp went straight to my cock.

"What do you want?" I asked.

This time he looked up and held my gaze. I wondered how much of the shyness was an act and how much was real.

"I think you know." The words were so quiet I could hardly hear them.

"Do I?"

"What do *you* want?" He sounded more confident now.

"Something I shouldn't take."

His lips curved up. "What if I want to give it to you, Daddy?"

I shivered and hoped he didn't notice. Damn, this boy was getting to me.

"You like that, huh?" he asked. "Daddy play."

I shrugged, not wanting to reveal too much. "A little, nothing too serious. What about you?" That was the truth. I liked to do Daddy/boy scenes, but it wasn't something I necessarily wanted to live full time.

"I'd like you to do something serious to my ass."

Oh, fuck. "That sounds promising. Would you be a good boy for me if I did?"

His eyes widened and he nodded. "Yes, Daddy."

Dear God, he was intoxicating. "And if you aren't?"

"Then you'll just have to teach me some discipline."

He licked his pink lips, and I had to clear my throat and force my brain to pull some words together. "I'll ask you one more time, boy. What do you want?"

He chewed his lip again, and I wondered how he still had any lipstick on. "I want you."

I looked down at the drink in his hand. We were already risking Carter and Felicity finding out. I didn't want him to have any other regrets. "How many of those have you had?"

"Enough to give me the courage to track you down and offer myself, but not enough to keep me from knowing what I want."

I smiled. "Good answer, boy."

"Thank you, Daddy."

I wanted to kiss the smirk right off his face. "That sassy mouth is going to get you in trouble."

"I'm counting on it."

Damn, he was hot. "I only give good boys what they ask for."

He chuckled, and I'd swear I could feel it in my dick. "I really do need a Daddy."

My mind was screaming for me to stop this before it went too far, but my cock was far more persuasive. "Tell me more. Tell me exactly what you want."

"I want you to put me on my knees and tell me what to do. I want to please you, give you whatever you need, and then…" He hesitated; the shyness he'd shown was back. His hands shook, and I didn't think it was an act now.

"And then?" I prompted.

"I want you to take care of me."

He was fucking perfect. "I'll take care of you, I promise, even when you're choking on my dick."

"Jesus. That's…" He practically swooned. I took his drink and set it and mine on a bench. Then I took his hand and tugged, encouraging him to walk with me. He laced his fingers in mine and gripped me hard, as if trying to mask the fact that his hand wasn't steady.

"Are you sure about this?" I asked.

He nodded, but he wouldn't look at me.

"Does it freak you out that I'm Carter's father?"

He frowned. "It should."

"But does it?"

"No."

"Look at me." When he did, I said, "I need you to be certain, and to tell me how hard you like to play."

"I like to be spanked, but I'm not a pain slut or anything. Most of all I like to be told what to do. I don't want to have to think. I just want to surrender. You can restrain me, but you don't have to. I'll stay where you put me. I can be so good."

I was so hard I worried that just the movement of fabric against my dick would make me come. I leaned down until our lips were almost touching. "I believe you. I think you're exactly what I'm looking for."

I kissed him before he could respond with words. He wrapped his arms around me, sliding them up my back as our tongues thrust against each other. He tasted so good, I didn't want to stop, but I heard voices nearby, so I pulled away.

"This is crazy," he said, and he was right.

"It is, but"—I took his hand and pressed it against my cock—"I want it anyway."

He squeezed me and I groaned. I was way too close to the edge. "Enough," I said, gripping his wrist and pulling him away. "How much longer do you need to stay at the reception?"

He frowned. "Not long, but I'll need to say goodnight to Felicity and Carter, and a few other people."

"I'll stay out here, and give you time. Then I'll say my own goodnights. I'll be upstairs in one hour, and I expect you to be in my suite, naked, with your ass lubed and stretched."

His mouth dropped open. "Christ."

"I thought you—"

"I do. That is like the hottest thing anyone has ever said to me."

"I'll have a lot more than that to say later, boy." I pulled out my wallet, found a key card, and handed it to him. I was really glad I'd kept both copies with me. "My room number is 344."

Avery ran his teeth over his lower lip as he took the card. Then he looked up through his absurdly long lashes. "Yes, Daddy. I'll be waiting."

"Don't disappoint me, boy." He sucked in his breath, proving that my words had the desired effect.

"I won't. I'll be the best boy you've ever had."

I didn't doubt that for a second.

CHAPTER FIVE

_____

AVERY

Once I'd stripped, I knelt on the plush carpet of Daddy's suite to see if it was as comfy as I thought it would be. The answer was hell yes. It was easily big enough for an orgy, which was kind of hot to think about even if I wasn't okay with Daddy sharing me. That was when I realized I didn't even know his first name. I'd had sex with guys whose names I didn't know before, but it had always been at a club or when someone knew where I was. I might be a bit of slut, but I was a safe one. Was I out of my mind to be here like this?

No. He wasn't really a stranger. He was Carter's father. And even with all the shit Carter's mom talked about him, I'd never heard anyone insinuate that he was dangerous. Still, was it a good idea to start with "Oh, Daddy, I'll do anything you tell me"? I usually thought a bit more carefully before submitting to more than a light spanking. But when I thought about him using That Voice and telling me what he wanted, I knew I was game for anything he wanted. Anything.

Okay, I had a few hard limits, but they'd never even come up before. So chances were Daddy wouldn't ask for anything I wasn't up for.

My roommate, Sean, was going to flip when I told him about this. Could I count on him not to tell

Felicity? Maybe. Yes. He didn't get the older guy thing, and he didn't even know about my Daddy fantasies. I mean, I thought he was pretty clear about the fact that I wanted a dominant man who liked taking care of me, but not that I played Daddy and boy occasionally. I didn't pretend I was actually a kid or anything. I just wanted to be a good boy so Daddy would be proud. I liked to be expected to obey when Daddy gave me orders. Of course if I told Sean the whole story, he'd probably think I was kidding and that it was actually the plot of some porno I'd watched. Because who ends up fucking the father of the groom at their best friend's wedding, kinky fucking, even? No one. That's who.

But this was real. I was sober enough not to doubt it. Since I'd planned to hit my favorite club after the reception wound down, I'd tried not to pregame overly much. It only took a few glasses of champagne for me to warm to the idea of tracking down Mr. Hillingdon and propositioning him. Now I didn't need to go looking for a hookup, because my hot daddy had ordered me to his room.

I wasn't going to disappoint him, so I grabbed the lube I'd set on a low table next to the ridiculously stylish sofa. I slicked up a few fingers and teased my ass, circling my hole before pushing in too fast and too hard for comfort, making my breath whoosh out. I even liked it rough from myself. I worked my fingers as deep as I could and imagined Daddy telling me what to do next. *Add another finger, boy. I need you good and open so my fat dick can slide right in there*. I moaned at the thought of him helping me, adding his fingers to mine, stuffing my ass so full. I wished I had a dildo. Did Daddy? I hoped so. Then he could stuff me with it while I choked on his dick.

My phone chimed, interrupting my fantasy. I glanced at it. I had a text from Felicity, thanking me again. I needed to respond, so I let my fingers slip from my ass. I was well stretched anyway. I quickly washed my hands and texted her back. I should feel guilty that I was about to do nasty things with her father-in-law, but I really didn't. It was just one night. Of course, if a man like him wanted more from me… No, I couldn't think about that. I'd be lucky if he just let me sleep here after we fucked.

> *I love you*
> *have an amazing honeymoon*
> *call me when you're back*

Felicity sent a heart emoji. Then I silenced my phone. I doubted Daddy liked for a boy's texts to interrupt him. Of course if my phone did chime while he was fucking me, I might need to be punished. His big hand would feel so good slapping my ass.

Fuck, if I didn't slow down on fantasizing, I might die from the ache in my cock before Daddy even got to the room. I glanced at the time. It had been fifty-five minutes since he'd told me he'd be there in an hour. Was he the kind of man who was exactly on time? I'd bet he was.

I paced the room, suddenly more nervous than I'd been since I'd approached him in the garden. I stared out the window. The suite had a nice view of the outdoor pools that connected to the spa, but I had to stay back enough that no one taking an evening soak got a full glimpse of my naked glory.

A few moments later, I heard footsteps in the hall. I ran to the middle of the room and knelt. Thank God I had, because the lock mechanism rattled and clicked. I took a deep breath as the door swung open.

Daddy's eyes widened when he saw me. He looked me up and down; his expression said he liked what he saw, and he couldn't wait to wreck me. I shivered.

"Did you do as you were told?"

I nodded, mouth too dry to speak.

"And you're ready to show me how good you can be?"

I swallowed and then said, "Yes, Daddy."

"Good." His smile turned evil. "Bend over. I want your forehead on the floor, ass in the air, and your hands clasped behind your back."

My heart pounded, and I hesitated for a second. Could I really expose myself to him like that?

"Boy?"

I did what he'd said, bending over and lifting my ass.

He circled me and then knelt behind me. His hand slid along my crack, then he circled my hole. "Nice and slick. I like that. You did listen."

"Yes, Daddy. I did exactly what you said."

I groaned when he pushed a finger into me.

"Mmm, yes, you did. How many fingers did you have in here?"

"Th-three." I was shaking just from him putting a finger in my ass.

"You wanted more, didn't you?"

How did he know? "Yeah, I did. I wanted to be stretched wide."

He chuckled, the sound so hot I had to bite my lip to hold in a whimper. "I bet you did. Are you a greedy boy who needs his ass stuffed?"

"I… um…"

He slapped my ass hard, making me jerk. "Answer me."

"Yes, I'm a slut for ass play."

He groaned, and I loved knowing I'd affected him. "Tonight you're my slut."

"Yes, Daddy."

"As long as you do what I say, you'll get what you need. And if I ask for too much, you'll say…"

"Red."

"Good boy." He pressed his thumb against my hole, circling, teasing, but not pushing in. I pressed my lips together to keep from begging for more.

"You told me earlier you don't need to be restrained, that all I have to do is tell you to stay still. Is that true?"

"Most of the time, but if you want… If you…"

"Shhh." He caressed my ass, and I vibrated with the need to push back against his hand, to have more of him. Maybe I would need him to tie me up. I'd never had anyone affect me quite like this.

He kept teasing me, caressing my tailbone and then drawing his fingers down my crack, brushing my taint, but not giving me any pressure. I rose up on my elbows, feeling desperate, but he pressed on the center of my back, pushing me back down.

"Relax into this. I'm going to play with your ass, and you're going to open up and let me."

I might if he'd just get on with it. "Yes, Daddy." I had to fight to keep my hips still.

"Stay still, boy. I'll be right back."

And he was, in seconds, with a pillow from the bed.

"Lift up."

I didn't think about obeying. I just did it. He laid the pillow on the floor, and I lowered myself again, ass in the air.

"Better, boy?" he asked as he rubbed circles on my back. "I don't want you getting rug burns on your face."

"Yes, thank you."

"I want you comfortable. I want this to feel good, but you will not come until I tell you."

"Yes, Daddy."

He chuckled, and I felt the sound deep in my balls. I had a feeling he was going to draw this out, torment me, and Jesus, I wanted that, but I was scared I would fail him. What was it about this man that made me desperate to please him?

He slid his hands from my shoulders to my ass, and I arched deeply, wiggling like a cat begging for attention.

He slapped my ass, making me yelp. "Stay still, boy. Just breathe and relax."

"Y-yes, Daddy."

He deepened his touch until it became a massage, digging into muscles that had been tense all day as I worried about the ceremony. I'd wanted everything to be perfect for Felicity. I couldn't hold back a moan as Daddy worked my lower back.

"Like that, boy?"

"Yes, it's so good."

"You needed this."

I nodded, already feeling floaty. He hadn't even started on my ass, but I was so relaxed. It was so easy with him, like I'd known him for ages, like we were meant to be.

But I couldn't start thinking like that. I would only end up disappointed.

When he dug his fingers into my ass cheeks and pulled them apart, I stopped being able to think. He brushed his thumbs over my hole one after the other. I writhed, unable to hold still anymore. The massage had somehow made my whole body extra sensitized.

Daddy laughed again. "Oh, this is going to be a lot of fun."

A muffled whimper was my only response.

"I need to get a few things from the bathroom. I want you to stay just like you are. I'll be right back, and I'll never leave the suite with you like this, okay?"

I trusted him to take care of me. "Yes, Daddy."

"Good boy."

He was back so fast I didn't even have time to get chilled. I heard the click of a lube bottle opening, then slick fingers pressed against my ass. I held my breath as he pushed two fingers—slowly, oh so slowly—into me.

"Breathe," he commanded.

I did, but my lungs felt tight, and the air whooshed back out quickly.

"I love how open you are for me."

He worked his fingers in and out, tormenting me, barely giving me anything and then taking even that away. He didn't change his rhythm or add another finger. He just kept relentlessly working me.

I squeezed the pillow and bit down on its softness. My cock was so hard I thought I would die. Seconds later, I broke. "Please, Daddy. Please give me more."

"Not yet. Good boys have to be patient."

This was too much. I couldn't stand it. "Daddy!"

He slapped my ass, and I wasn't sure if it hurt or felt good. I was so mixed up and from nothing but a few fingers in my ass.

He kept going, and I tried to breathe slowly, to force myself to relax. I started to sink into the discomfort. Finally, he added another finger and the stretch was delicious. He twisted his wrist, and I whimpered and pushed back against him. He didn't scold me that time. He started moving a little faster, but it still wasn't enough, and he never went deep enough to brush my sweet spot.

"You want more, don't you, boy?"

"Yes. Yes, please." I'm not sure I even knew what I was saying at this point. He'd already taken me further than most men I'd played with, and we'd hardly done anything. I was sure there was a puddle of precum under me, and my dick was ready to go off at the slightest touch.

He pushed in deeper, and his pinky slid into me too, intensifying the stretch. "Oh, fuck. I… Fuck."

"You can take it, boy, just relax."

I could. I'd had that much before, but he was flexing his fingers and rotating them, screwing into me. It was so good, even though it burned like fire. Then he hit *that* spot, and I cried out. Half whine, half scream. I sounded like an animal, a very desperate animal. The embarrassment of it only made me harder.

"Oh, fuck. You do like that." He added more lube and kept working me, trying to open up his fingers even as my ass clamped down on them.

"Jesus. Fuck. I… I need."

"Hush, baby." He rubbed my back as he kept going. I felt like I was being split in two, but God help me, I wanted more. I wanted to hurt.

"Have you ever been fisted?"

Heat filled my face. "No."

"You've thought about it, though."

So much. "Yes, Daddy."

He pushed in just a bit farther, and I felt his thumb brush against me. I tensed. Was he? "I don't—"

He pulled back. "Easy. It's okay. I would never try that the first night with anyone. Or the second. But it's something to think about."

"Yes." The word was a whisper, but I thought he'd heard it.

Then it hit me. Was he saying he wanted to see me again? And maybe again after that?

I started to panic, but he pushed back in. "You can fantasize about it now, though, about me pushing deeper, stretching you beyond what you think you can take, making you hurt while you beg for more, for my whole arm up your ass."

Jesus Christ. That shouldn't be so hot. I'd thought I was right on the edge before, but when he flexed his fingers, I nearly came.

"Don't you dare." How did he know?

He pressed against my prostate then. Fuck, he was merciless. I fought the need to spill, to just let go. Then slowly, so slowly, he pulled his fingers from my ass. "That's good, boy. Very good."

I was panting. Ready to beg, ready to do anything to have more. "Daddy, please."

"What do you need, boy?"

"You." I wasn't sure I had the capacity to say more. He'd nearly wrecked me.

"I'm right here."

"Your cock… Inside me… I need. So empty now."

He pulled my ass cheeks apart. "Mmm, yes. You're wide open for me. I'm going to slide right into your ass."

"Please, Daddy. Fuck me."

"Or… maybe I'll just jerk off and let my spunk fall right into your open hole."

"No, please. I'll be good. I'll do whatever you want."

He chuckled, a low, evil sound that made my cock jump. My balls were so tight I didn't know how I'd keep from coming as soon as he entered me.

He dragged his slick fingers over my taint, and I stiffened. If he touched my cock… He cupped my balls and squeezed, not hard enough to really hurt, but there was an edge of pain. I help my breath, not knowing what he wanted from me. He rolled my balls in his hand and then tugged.

I whined, a desperate sound.

"I love the noises you make, boy. Don't you dare hold any of them back."

"Please." I wasn't sure of what I was asking for anymore.

"You're just as delicious as I thought you'd be." He let go of my sac and circled my entrance with the tip of a finger.

If hc didn't fuck me I was going to lose my mind.

"Head down."

I rested my head on my folded arms and heard the sound of a condom wrapper tearing. I looked under my arm and saw that he hadn't bothered to undress.

He'd just opened his pants and pulled his cock out. Damn, that was hot.

When Daddy caught me peeking, he reached under me and wrapped a hand around my cock.

"Don't come." My body went rigid when he stroked. I was too close—this was impossible. I didn't want to come, I wanted to please him. I had to.

Finally, he let me go.

"Breathe, boy," he ordered, laying a hand at the base of my spine.

I did, but my breaths were ragged. My whole body quaked with need.

"I'm proud of you, boy. That wasn't easy, was it?"

"No, Daddy."

"If you obey me, you won't have to suffer anymore."

But I would. Because once he started fucking me, I wasn't going to be able to hold back.

"Boy?"

"Yes, Daddy?"

"I'm going to put a cock ring on you now, because I want to fuck you hard and deep for a good long time."

I exhaled, so relieved. "Thank you, Daddy."

His hand gripped me again. I expected him to tease me, but he snapped the ring in place without touching me more than necessary.

"Thank you." The words came out like an exhale.

"You're welcome, boy. I'm here to take care of you, remember that."

"Yes, Daddy. I need that. I need someone to take care of me." And I did. I wasn't just role-playing now. I needed this badly. Tears stung my eyes as he brushed my ass with the tip of his cock.

"Don't hold back anything you're feeling, boy. I want all of you, all your emotions, okay?"

"I…" I made a choked sound. I was going to cry. I couldn't hold it back.

"You don't have to be embarrassed with me, boy. I'll take you where you need to go."

I believed him. I didn't even really know him, but I believed him. Somehow he knew what I needed.

He pushed into me, not stopping until he was fully seated. It felt so good to be full of him, so like home.

"Feel that, boy? That's me claiming you, owning you. You like being Daddy's boy?"

"Yes. Oh, God, yes. Please."

He pulled out and then drove back in so hard, I slid along the mattress.

"More," I cried, and he gave it to me, slamming his hips against my ass. I bit my lip as tears ran down my cheeks.

"Boy, I told you not to hold back anything."

I sobbed then, letting it all out as he fucked me relentlessly, just like he'd promised. I cried and moaned and spoke nonsense until the world around us faded. There was just Daddy and his cock and my need. I was so close. If I hadn't had the ring I would've come already, disgracing myself.

"So good. Such a good boy." He petted me, and I pushed into his touch.

A few seconds later, he pulled all the way out.

"No!" I shouted before I could stop myself.

"Turn over, boy," he said, his voice soothing. He seemed to know how far gone I was, how little control I had left.

I flopped onto my back and looked up into his dark eyes.

His cock bobbed in front of him, thick and red. I wanted it in my mouth. I wanted to worship it.

He reached down and removed the ring from my cock.

"Jerk yourself off while I watch."

My hand was around my dick before he finished speaking. I gasped as I slid my hand along my length. I was so hard it hurt.

"Eyes on me."

"Yes, Daddy." I met his gaze, and it was so intense, like he could see into me. But I'd already sobbed like a child as he'd fucked me, what else could he see that was worse than that?

I worked my cock, tightening my grip. I cried out, mouth dropping open as I shot so hard, cum hit my chin. My orgasm went on and on until I thought there couldn't be anything left. Then Daddy took his cock in his hand, and my body jerked once more.

"I want to see you covered in my cum, boy."

"Yes, please. I love that. Come on me."

He worked himself, and I lifted my legs so he could move closer. He growled as he stroked himself, and then, with a roar, he came. His release splashed on top of mine, and I wanted to rub it into my skin. I wanted to wear his mark, his scent. I was so fucked up over this man.

He collapsed on top of me when he finished. I wrapped my legs around him and slid my fingers into his sweat-damp hair. Then I closed my eyes and sank into the floor, wanting to hold onto this moment for as long as I could. Because no matter what he'd said in the heat of the moment, I was sure once he came to his senses, I'd be out the door headed home.

CHAPTER SIX

GRAHAM

I scooped Avery up and carried him to the bathroom. He was so blissed out, he was limp in my arms, his breathing shallow, but there was a goofy smile on his face. I hoisted him up so his head was on my shoulder. "Are you okay?"

"Mmm" was all he said. For now I'd take that as a yes.

"I'm going to wrap you in a towel so you don't get cold while I start a shower."

"So good to me."

I kissed the top of his head. "You were amazing, and now I'll take care of you, boy."

"You can send me home now, Daddy."

He didn't really want that, did he? "You're staying with me, at least until you're recovered."

"Y-you'd let me stay?"

Let him? "I want you to stay."

He burrowed into me and sighed. I hoped what we were doing was okay. He'd seemed to go really deep into subspace, and now he was barely conscious. I'd known there was something between us, something more than just hookup lust, but I'd never expected things to go so far. I hope he wouldn't be freaked out when he came back to himself.

I stroked Avery's hair, pushing it off his forehead. I couldn't stop looking at him. He was intoxicating, and I'd pushed him more than I ever had someone I'd just met. He'd been glorious as he'd fought to hold still and begged for more. And when he came, crying out, body spasming again and again, he was fucking beautiful.

I probably should send him home once I knew he was okay, but I didn't want to. I wasn't sure I'd even be ready to give him up after an entire night together. But I had to, didn't I? He was Felicity's best friend and at least close to the same age as my son. Carter trusted me now. I couldn't do something that might fuck that up.

But despite the way Avery felt against me, under me, there was so much more here than just sex. We'd connected in a way I hadn't with other partners. I wanted this part, the caretaking, as much as I'd wanted to fuck him.

I sat Avery down on the stool by the vanity and laid a thick, fluffy towel over his shoulders, then I started the shower so the water could heat up.

"Avery?"

"Hmm?"

I wasn't sure he was actually awake, so I cupped his face and made him look at me. "Baby, you need to take your makeup off."

"Oh… um… yeah. Bad for my skin to leave it on."

"Do you have something for that? You shouldn't just use soap, right?"

"Yeah, it's in my bag."

I hurried out to the sitting area and grabbed his bag. When I handed it to him, his fingers fumbled with the zipper, so I opened it for him. "Tell me what to get."

"There's a packet of wipes in there, and a purple bottle that says eye makeup remover."

I found both. "Now tell me what to do."

He reached for the wipes. "I can do it."

"No, I'm doing this. I'm taking care of you."

"O-okay. Use the wipes first. They'll clean off most of it, but you'll need to put the stuff in the bottle on a cotton ball to get my mascara and eyeliner off."

I moved the stool so he could lean back against the wall and look up at me. "Relax and let me clean you up."

"Love your voice," he murmured.

I glanced down and saw the cum drying on his stomach. "You look so fucking hot like this." I ran my fingers over his torso.

"Mmm. You covered me in cum."

"I couldn't help myself."

He smiled. "I'm glad you did."

Not sure I could handle where this conversation was going, I pulled one of the wipes from the package and began cleaning his face. He closed his eyes, but I could feel him smiling under my hand as I wiped away his lipstick. I wet a cotton ball with the liquid remover and gently ran it over his eyelids.

"You can rub harder. It won't hurt." But I didn't, I worked him gently, and his breathing quickened. I looked down and saw that he was half hard. "How do you have any energy left?"

He laughed. "I'm always horny. Don't you remember being twenty-five?"

"Don't you dare make an old man joke."

Now he was full-on giggling. "I wouldn't. I swear."

I kissed him, pressing my lips to his, giving him time to open his mouth. His arms came around my neck and I cupped his face, wanting to show him how careful I could be with him if he needed that.

"So good." He spoke against my lips, and I felt more than heard the words.

"Yeah, it is." I took his hand and pulled him to his feet.

"I'm going to clean you now, and then I'll put you to bed."

"Okay, Daddy."

I undressed quickly while Avery watched me, eyes growing wider. "So hot, Daddy."

His words had my dick doing its best to rise again. We stepped into the shower, and I soaped up a cloth and washed him all over. Then I squirted shampoo into my hand and massaged his head as I worked it into his hair. When I was done, he was nearly as limp as he'd been when I'd scooped him off the floor. I was thankful for the bench in this enormous shower. I sat him on it as I quickly washed myself. Then I helped him out and wrapped him in a towel.

When we were both dry, I gave his ass a gentle slap to encourage him to move. "Come on. Let's go to bed."

"You really want me to stay?"

I hated how uncertain he looked. "I want to wrap myself around you and keep you safe."

"Oh, Daddy. I want that too."

Good. I led him to the bedroom, then I pulled back the sheets, and he climbed in. I spooned around him, and in a few moments, he was sound asleep. I lay

47

awake far longer, trying to tell myself that no matter how crazy this was, this thing between us was real, and worth any risk.

CHAPTER SEVEN

AVERY

When I woke the next morning, I tried to turn over and winced. Damn, I was sore. But as memories of the night before flooded my mind, I smiled. It was soooo worth it. I shifted, snuggling closer to the heavy warm body beside me. He grunted and wrapped an arm around me, pulling me tight against him. He mumbled something, but I couldn't understand it. I wasn't sure how awake he actually was. I let him drift back to sleep, because I had a feeling I wouldn't be staying long once he woke up.

I was thrilled that he'd wanted me to stay the night, but he hadn't given me any reason to think this went beyond a hot—really damn hot—evening of role play. That was what I'd expected, after all, and it should have been fine. But what I'd felt with him, the way he'd broken me down and then put me back together, was unbelievably perfect. I'd played Daddy and boy before, but this felt different. I felt like he could actually be that something more that I'd been craving, a man who'd take care of me, treat me like someone to be cherished, not just fucked. Why did he have to be Carter's dad? What would Felicity say if she found out? Would Carter be angry? Would it fuck things up between him and his dad? I didn't want to jeopardize what they'd finally found.

49

Haven't you already?

No. There was no reason for Carter and Felicity to find out about last night. As much as I wanted to stay, I knew I couldn't. Slipping out from under Daddy's arm wasn't easy. Damn, the man was strong.

When I sat up, I glanced back at him and sighed. He was so fucking hot. I'd likely see him again sometime at Carter and Felicity's house, and that would just suck. Or… Maybe he and I could—No, this had to be it.

I turned away and stood.

"If you're getting up, it better be to order us room service."

I sputtered. "Wh-what?"

"You heard me, boy."

He expected me to stay for breakfast? "But I was… I thought."

"I'm hungry, and I'm sure you are too. A boy needs to eat after Daddy wears him out."

Oh my God. He still wanted to play. "Um…" Apparently my brain was fried.

"Boy?"

"Yes, Daddy?"

"Do you need a spanking? I thought your ass would be sore enough from last night."

I hesitated for a second. A spanking sounded almost as good as breakfast. "What would you like me to order, Daddy?"

He smiled then. "Bacon, eggs, and toast for me. And coffee. Lots of coffee. Order whatever you want for yourself, as long as you have some protein. You'll need your strength today."

"I…" This couldn't really be happening.

He reached out and took my hand. "You know you can still use your safe word any time, right? It can apply to anything you're uncomfortable with. I would never try to keep you here if you wanted to go."

I exhaled slowly. "I want to stay. I'm just a bit overwhelmed. I didn't think you'd want more than what we did last night."

He rose onto his knees and stroked my hair. I leaned into the warm touch. It felt so good to be taken care of, to be soothed.

"I want you. More than I probably should. I was hoping you'd be here when I woke up, because I'm staying until Monday, and I want you to spend the weekend with me."

"I…" This was way more than I'd expected, and if I didn't want to leave now, ending things after two more nights wasn't going to be any easier. But how could I say no?

I looked down into his dark eyes that were filled with heat. "I'd like that."

"Good. Daddy needs more time to take care of his boy."

"Mmm. That sounds amazing, but…" Was I really going to bring this up and potentially ruin everything? Yes. Yes, I was. "What about Carter?"

He stiffened. "I'll deal with Carter."

"Y-you're not going to tell him, are you?"

"No. Not unless…"

My pulse thundered in my ears. "Unless?"

"Never mind. He doesn't need to know. I'm having lunch with him and Felicity today, but after that they'll be leaving for Trinidad. You can hang out here while I'm gone, or go do whatever you need to."

What had he been going to say? Unless he asks? Unless we keep seeing each other? "Okay, that… that sounds fine."

"And once I'm done, we'll go to the spa."

"I don't have an appointment. I'm not sure—"

"You'll be my guest," he said. "I'm fairly persuasive." That was an understatement. "I bet I can even get them to fit you in for a massage."

Heat rushed to my face. I'd bought a lot of new makeup and clothes lately. I wasn't sure I could afford the spa. "Um… I don't know how much—"

"My treat."

"I can't let you do that."

"I want to do this for you. Daddy takes care of his boy, remember?"

I frowned. "I don't want that to extend to paying for me. That's not—"

He held up his hands. "I'm sorry. I didn't mean to cross a line. I'll enjoy an afternoon at the spa a lot more if I have a friend with me. This is a no-strings-attached offer. If you meet another man by the pool, feel free to swim off with him."

"You wouldn't care?"

"Oh, I'd care, but I wouldn't stop you. You don't owe me anything."

"Okay." This whole thing was like a fantasy come to life. It was so good, so perfect it was almost scary. As much as I loved the game we were playing, I wasn't sure how long we could sustain it.

"Um…" How should I ask? Did Daddy only want me because I was willing to play this game?

"Don't be shy. You can say anything to me, boy."

"I was wondering if we could… um… drop the role play while we eat breakfast. I'm not sure—"

He laid a hand on my arm. "Yes. I couldn't keep it up the whole weekend anyway. Let's just be us and talk over breakfast. We'll work out what feels right after that, okay?"

"Yeah. I'd like that."

"Good. Now I'm going to get in the shower, and you should call in our order."

As he walked to the bathroom, I stared, taking in the sight of his gorgeous body and round ass. Then I realized I didn't know how he liked his eggs.

"Daddy?"

He turned around, brows raised. "I thought we were going to drop the role-play?"

"We are, but if I have to call you Mr. Hillingdon I might as well—"

"Graham. My name is Graham."

Suddenly, I felt more shy than I ever had last night. "Hi."

He smiled softly. "Hi."

***

"So how long have you known Felicity?" Graham asked once we'd each made a serious dent in our breakfasts.

"Since kindergarten. She wore this big puffy dress on the first day. Some stupid kid made fun of her, and I broke all his crayons."

Graham snickered. "You must have formed quite a bond."

"We did. We've been through a lot together. I… I don't know how I would've gotten through high school without her."

"Were you out then?"

I nodded. "I… Well, the way I am, people just assumed I was gay before I said anything. I had plenty of accepting friends, but lots of people gave me shit too. And some liked to complain that I was too gay. They'd tell me that if I'd just tone it down, things would be easier for me."

Graham laid a hand over mine. "I'm sorry."

I shrugged. "That was years ago; things are much better now. Felicity always defended me, and she helped me learn not to care so much what people think." I still took shit for who I was, but it bothered me a hell of a lot less.

"Good. I haven't gotten to know Felicity very well, but she seems like an amazing woman."

"She is. Carter is very lucky."

"I'm so happy for him and happy to have been a part of all this."

Now it was my turn to squeeze his hand. "I'm glad you're here too, and not just because of"— I waved my hand around—"This, but because you deserve to have a relationship with your children. And stepping in to help Mandy. That was… That was awesome."

His expression softened. "Thank you. My kids mean a lot to me."

"Are you sure whatever this thing is we're doing is okay? I don't want to make things awkward for you?"

He shook his head. "I love my kids, but they don't dictate my life."

That sounded very reasonable, but I wondered if he would be that rational if Carter found out what was going on and freaked.

"So you've done this before, the Daddy/boy thing?" Graham asked before taking a sip of coffee.

I swirled the last of my French toast in a puddle of syrup as I decided how to answer that. "I have, but it's just been like a scene, not…" Real? No, that couldn't be right.

"This intense?"

"Yeah, and this… like it really works, like it's so easy to pretend I almost forget that's what I'm doing." My heart was beating so hard, I thought it might jump out of my chest. "Is that… Does that… scare you?"

He shook his head. "No, because that's exactly how I felt."

"Oh, wow. Just so you know, I didn't want to take a break because I wasn't enjoying it, but because I was enjoying it too much."

He grinned. "That's… I think I liked it too much too. This is fast, and maybe a little scary. I think this break was good. I'm not sure I'd ever want to role play all the time, to truly live it, but this has been the most real game I've ever played."

Oh my God. "Me too."

We didn't talk for several moments. We both ate, and I assumed he was trying to process what we'd shared like I was.

As I finished my last piece of bacon, I watched Graham spread jam on a piece of toast. He must have felt my attention because he looked up and our gazes locked. "What do you want, Avery?"

I started to pretend I didn't want anything, that I was just enjoying the view. Instead, I said, "I want to suck your cock."

Graham set the toast down, pushed his chair back from the table, and opened his legs. "Then come do it."

My pulse sped up. I was finally going to get that beautiful cock in my mouth. I slipped from my chair, going to my knees and walking on them until I reached him, not because I thought he expected it, but because it was the fastest way to get to what I wanted.

I pushed his robe apart and licked my lips as I looked down at his half-hard cock. "You seem at least somewhat interested."

He growled and brought a hand to the back of my head. "Stop talking and get to work."

So some of that dominance wasn't role play at all. I brought my hands together at the base of my spine and leaned forward into his lap. Using only my mouth, I drew him in and sucked. His cock swelled more, and I loved the feel of him hardening in my mouth. He kept one hand on my head and gripped the arm of his chair with the other. I couldn't see it well, but I was sure his knuckles were going white as I teased him with my tongue. He hardened more, almost choking me, it happened so fast.

"Yes," he hissed. When he was all the way hard, I opened my throat and devoured him until my nose brushed his pubes. I held him there as long as I could. Then I pulled back slowly and let him drop from my mouth.

His cock bobbed in front of me, and he wrapped his hand around it and dragged it over my lips. I pushed my tongue into the slit. And then I opened again. This time he brought both hands to my face and pulled me onto his length, not forcing me, just making it clear what he wanted. I worked him, bobbing up and down, using tongue and a hint of teeth until his breaths were harsh and he moaned for me. I loved the rush this gave me. Even like this, with my hands behind my back, on my knees, nearly choking on his width, I had power over him. And in that moment, I loved it. I could make him come apart. Despite how strong he was, how I needed him to take care of me, I could give him this release.

"Gonna come, boy."

I took him deeper, and looked up at him, trying to let him know I wanted him to.

"More," he growled, and I gave more. Sucking him so hard he probably felt like his balls were going to come out through his dick.

"Yes!" His hands tightened around me. "Fuck, yes."

He shot down my throat, and I swallowed frantically, not wanting to spill a drop, but there was too much for me. When he finished, I licked my lips and chin, moaning at the taste of him.

He grabbed my upper arms and pulled me up so he could lick off what I missed. Then he ravished me hard, sucking my lips, driving his tongue into me.

"That was incredible," he whispered against my lips. "So good. Fucking perfect."

Those words did even more to me than sucking his dick had. I hadn't realized how deep my need-to-please kink went, but he pressed all the right buttons. I pushed my robe aside so I could get to my cock. I needed to come, and I needed it now, but he grabbed my wrist and shook his head.

"Not yet. I love how wound up you get when you're forced to slow down."

"But—"

His glare made me freeze.

"I thought… I thought we weren't…"

His expression softened. "If you don't want to, tell me. I'll suck you or jack you off, or…"

I did want it. I wanted everything. "I want whatever you do, Daddy."

He sucked in his breath. "Do you have any clothes here besides your tux?"

"Yes, I have what I'd planned to wear out after the reception and the clothes I wore over here yesterday."

"You're going to shower and dress in something that's not insanely conspicuous, but before you dress, I have a surprise for you."

"A surprise?"

He nodded.

"What kind of surprise?"

"You'll find out when you're clean and I'm dressed."

He was going to be the death of me. "Yes, Daddy."

CHAPTER EIGHT

GRAHAM

After Avery came out of the shower, I fought the urge to grab him, turn him around, and bend him over the bed. Eventually I would do exactly that, but I wanted him to dress me first.

"Open the drawers and find some jeans for me. I'm going to choose a shirt and then I want you to dress me."

By the time he'd helped me into my pants and was buttoning my shirt, my cock was swelling again despite how hard I'd come from his blowjob. I had a feeling I'd be spending most of the weekend at least half hard. Avery was simply too delectable.

He kept glancing up at me every few seconds as he buttoned my shirt, as if making sure I was pleased.

"You're doing a wonderful job," I reassured him.

He smiled and his eyes lit up. His reaction to praise warmed me all over.

"Now tuck it in."

I held myself still, knowing that feeling him touch my ass as he pushed the shirttails into my pants might kill me, especially since I wasn't going to fuck him again any time soon.

As Avery slipped his hands into the front of my pants, he pressed the heel of his hand against my dick, and it was all I could do not to arch into his touch. I was torn between scolding him and showing him just how stoic I could be about it.

Then he did it again, and there was no way in hell I could pretend I was unaffected. I grabbed his wrist. "Don't touch me without permission, boy."

His eyes widened. "Yes, Daddy. I'm sorry."

He looked so nervous that I smirked to let him know I was teasing. "Hurry up and finish so I can show you the surprise."

He sank his teeth into his lower lip as he fastened my pants and buckled my belt. And damn if I didn't consider changing my mind about fucking. I could always put a ring on him and not let him come. No, I would stick with my plan.

When he was finished, I took a step back, needing a moment before I touched him. "Turn around and bend over the bed."

"Daddy?"

"When I told you I had a surprise for you, maybe I should have said it was for your ass."

His mouth dropped open.

"I'm waiting."

"Sorry, Daddy." He obeyed, stretching out over the end of the bed.

I unzipped my suitcase, reached into one of the zippered compartments, and pulled out a vibrating butt plug. It wasn't huge, but it was a decent size. More importantly, it had a remote control, which I intended to make good use of while Avery and I took a walk around the hotel grounds.

I held the plug and remote where Avery could see them. "This is a vibrating plug. I want to put it inside you and have you wear it until I'm back from lunch. You're not to touch yourself, and when I'm with you I may use the remote at any time."

He swallowed audibly as he looked up at me from the bed.

"Do you consent?"

His shock turned to a smile. "Yes. Oh my God, yes."

I'd guessed right. He was totally into the idea of me controlling him like that. "If you tell me to take it out, I will, okay?"

He nodded. "I don't think I'll need to, though. Like I said last night, I'm a total slut for things in my ass."

"That's exactly what I like in a boy."

He grinned, but his expression turned wary when I switched the plug on and he saw how strong the vibrations could get.

"You won't turn it up that far, will you?"

I shrugged. "That depends on what I think you need."

He whined a bit. "I think I'm going to love and hate this."

"I think you are too. Now, hold your ass open for me."

Avery reached behind himself and pulled his ass cheeks apart. I longed to lick his hole, but once I got started rimming him, I wasn't going to want to stop. I squirted lube on the plug and rubbed it around. "I sterilized it thoroughly at home, okay?"

"Yes, Daddy."

"I'll always take care of my boy."

He nodded. "Thank you."

"I want to put this in without any prep. Can you take that, boy?"

He squirmed a bit. "Yes. Please, Daddy. I, um… I like that."

"I had a feeling you did."

I pushed the tip into him and he tensed. I teased the rim of his hole with a slick finger and squirted more lube on the plug. "Push out, baby."

He exhaled, and I drove the plug farther in.

He bucked like he was trying to escape it. "Fuck, that hurts."

I gave him more.

"Oh, God. Yes. Please."

"You like how it hurts?"

He nodded. I gave a hard push, forcing him to take the widest part of the plug.

He whimpered, but he didn't protest further. Then I hit the remote and he cried out, his body jerking. I slapped his ass. "Stay still."

"How the fuck can I with this thing buzzing in my ass?"

I spanked him hard. "Boy, you better apologize."

He seemed to suddenly realize what he'd said. "I'm sorry, Daddy. It's…"

I turned the vibration up and he writhed, working himself against the bed. "Fuck, oh fuck!"

"Don't you dare come."

When I shut it off, he sagged against the mattress, panting.

I rubbed his ass. "I'm going to enjoy this a lot."

"Thank you, Daddy. I like my surprise."

Those soft words did more for me than seeing him fighting the sensations the plug gave him. No way was I going to be able to let him go on Monday, but now wasn't the time to discuss that. I needed him to get used to this, to us.

"Get dressed. We're going to explore the rose garden. I want to see the different varieties in the daylight."

"We're what?"

I raised a brow.

"You want me to go outside with this?" He gestured toward his ass.

I spanked him again, right on top of the handprint that still showed.

He tried to swallow his whimper, and I glared at him. "You will not deprive me of any of those delicious noises, and if you complain again, you won't come at all today."

He jumped up from the bed. "I'm sorry. I'll get dressed now, and we'll go wherever you'd like."

"Much better, boy."

A few moments later, Avery was dressed and looking decidedly uncomfortable about his situation. I brushed my thumb over his lips. "I miss the lipstick."

"Oh. I can put some on if you want me to."

"That's up to you. I want you to be comfortable."

He raised his brows. "Seriously?"

"Comfortable about how you present yourself. Otherwise…"

"Right." He headed to the bathroom. "If you want lipstick, I'm happy to give you that."

"Can I watch?"

He frowned. "You're asking permission?"

"Of course, if you don't want me in here—"

63

"You just put a dildo up my ass. You have a remote for it in your pocket, and you're asking if you can watch me put on lipstick?"

"You can choose to have privacy from me anytime. Consenting to one thing isn't agreeing to me owning you, no matter what I might say in the heat of the moment."

"I like you saying you own me when we play. And I don't mind if you watch me now."

"All right." I rubbed the back of his neck with my thumb, and he leaned into the touch.

He reached into the bag I'd brought him the night before and pulled out a zippered pouch. When he opened it, at least six different lipsticks rolled out. He grabbed several more as well and held them up. "Pick one."

I stared at them, thinking of how they'd look on his lips. I wanted to see them all. But finally, I selected one that was fuck-me red.

He laughed. "I knew you'd pick that one."

"Why?"

"Because it looks best on lips you want around your cock."

I chuckled. "Then you should have put it on earlier."

"Oh, I'm planning to suck you again. And again. And—"

"Get on with it."

"Primer first," he said.

He pulled out another tube, squeezed some gel onto his finger and rubbed it on his lips, then he pulled out a pencil and outlined them. They already looked fuller, and damn if I didn't want them right back on my dick. When he filled the color in, I realized my mouth was hanging open. How the hell was watching him do that so sexy?

He rubbed his lips together and did an exaggerated air kiss. Then he glanced at me coyly. "Eyeliner too?"

I reached into my pocket and hit the remote.

He made a beautiful sound and gripped the counter. His eyes closed, and he chewed his lower lip. I could tell he was fighting the urge to squirm. I waited until he gave in and started rocking his hips back and forth before I turned off the vibrations.

"Holy fuck!"

I gave him an assessing stare. "You'll have to have more control when we're in public."

"I… I'm not sure I can do this."

"I won't turn it up that high in the garden. At least not at first."

"Daddy," he whined.

"You're adorable when you pout."

His eyes narrowed.

"Do you really want me to take it out?"

He looked at me, then back at himself in the mirror, then at me again. "No."

I laid a hand on his shoulder. "Thank you for being willing to try for me."

"You're welcome, Daddy."

"I want eyeliner too."

I watched as he finished with his makeup. One day I'd have to play with him while he put it on, see how far I could push him before he couldn't keep his hand steady. And then I'd… Okay, if I wasn't going to bend him over the counter right now, I had to stop thinking along those lines.

I held out my hand. "Let's go."

He smiled, those red lips looking especially wicked. "I'm glad you want to spend the day with me."

I wanted to spend forever with him. Ridiculous, maybe, but true. "I'm glad you agreed to stay." I tugged him off the stool. "No more stalling. I want to see just how much control my boy has."

"Oh, fuck."

***

How had I thought I could pay attention to rose varieties with Avery beside me, walking stiffly and occasionally biting his lip as if holding in a whimper because the dildo shifted to hit him just right. He paused and leaned down to smell a rose, and like the bastard I was, I reached into my pocket and pressed the remote.

Avery gasped just as an elderly couple stepped into the garden. He looked at me with a pleading expression, but I had no mercy. I left the vibrations on until they walked by. I didn't think they'd paid any attention to us, but Avery didn't know that. He'd been too busy turning away and squeezing his eyes shut.

When I walked up behind him and put my arms around him, he stiffened.

"What if Carter—"

"You really think they're going to leave their room before they meet me for lunch?"

"I don't know. I—"

"Shhh." I kissed his neck and he shuddered.

"Tell me how that felt."

"Embarrassing."

I nibbled his neck and he sighed, leaning into me. I could really get used to this. "Tell me more."

"It's like my whole body is electrified, like the sensations are literally going all the way to my fingertips, my toes, the top of my head."

"Mmm. Perfect."

"Bastard."

"Do you really want to go there, boy?"

He sucked in his breath, and I ran my tongue along the outer edge of his ear.

Footsteps echoed along one of the paths.

"Someone's coming," he hissed.

"I know."

"Oh, God, please don't—"

"Then talk. Tell me everything about how you felt just then."

"I felt humiliated, like those people walking by knew what you were doing to me, and fuck me, I loved it."

I laughed into his hair. "I thought you did."

"It's like I'm so embarrassed, so sure they can hear the plug buzzing, and yet, it's so hot and the embarrassment gets mixed up with the sensations, and I'm just so turned on."

"Mmmhmm."

"You're awfully smug about this."

"Damn right I am."

"Can we—"

I turned the plug on again. He stiffened and glared at me, but I could see the lust in his eyes.

"Let's walk."

He looked truly horrified. "I… I can't."

"Yes, you can. Because I want you to."

I only continued the torment for a few steps. When I hit the remote, I saw the tension leave him. I took his hand and smiled at him. "I'm proud of you, boy."

He shivered. "Thank you."

I squeezed his hand, and we walked until it was time for me to meet Carter and Felicity. I led Avery into a secluded area of the garden. He looked apprehensive, and I almost ordered him to his knees, but that was more of a risk than I wanted to take. Also it wasn't something I'd ask for without discussing his limits more first. I had no reason to think he was seriously into exhibitionism. "I want you to head back up to my room. You're not allowed to touch yourself or to adjust the plug in any way. Is that clear?"

He nodded. "Yes, Daddy."

"Good. Feel free to order anything you'd like from room service. After lunch, I'll join you, and if you've been a good boy, I'll reward you for how well you did out here."

"I'll be good. I promise."

I'd be rewarding myself too. I doubted he was any harder than I was. "Go on."

"You aren't walking in with me?"

I shook my head. "No, I need a few minutes."

He grinned. His red lips made me reconsider asking him to blow me right here.

"I thought you were going to be a good boy."

"Yes, Daddy." The smirk on his face told a different story.

As he walked away, I hit the remote and watched him stumble. He moved slowly, glancing around to see if anyone was watching. I thought about making him walk all the way to the door like that, but I relented. He paused when the vibrations stopped, probably trying to catch his breath. I kept my eyes on him as he started moving again and disappeared inside.

I was going home in less than forty-eight hours. Would Avery agree to see me again? If he did, would he insist on keeping our relationship hidden? I didn't want to hide. I'd fucked up my life by lying to my kids, my wife, myself. I'd finally won Carter's trust. I wouldn't lose it now; even if he was pissed at me for my choices, they would be choices that were out in the open.

CHAPTER NINE

GRAHAM

Carter and Felicity couldn't take their eyes off each other as we started our lunch. But I didn't care if they just gazed at each other and ignored me for the rest of the meal. I was thankful to have been able to share in their moment.

After finishing most of his fries, Carter finally turned to face me. "Thank you for meeting us. I wish we'd gotten more time together yesterday."

"Yesterday was about you. I'm just here to support you."

"You've been fantastic," Felicity said. "We really appreciate it."

I really hadn't done much other than make a few calls and gift them their honeymoon, which was easy for me. There was no point in having the money I did if I wasn't going to use it to make other people happy.

Carter seemed to lose himself in Felicity's eyes again. "If I had any doubt you two were a perfect match, this weekend would have ended it."

Felicity laughed. "Could you tell Avery that? I think he's still a bit skeptical."

I made a strangled sound and tried to cover it with a cough. "Avery? Um… Why would he listen to me? I don't even know him." Oh, shit. That sounded way too forced.

Carter gave me an odd look.

"Of course, if I see him, I'll tell him." That wasn't any more natural. I needed to just shut up. They were both looking at me like they were trying to figure out if I was drunk.

"You seem a bit… distracted," Carter said. "Are you sleeping okay? I thought the beds here were amazing." He must have realized immediately how that sounded. His face turned red and his mouth dropped open. "I didn't mean… just that they're good for sleeping."

I laughed. "I understand, and you're right. They are very nice beds."

"Of course, having a comfy bed doesn't necessarily mean a person will get a lot of sleep," Felicity said.

Carter turned even redder.

"She's right," I said. "Sometimes there simply isn't much time for sleep."

"Dad!" Carter said, and the people at the next table turned to look at him.

Felicity narrowed her eyes, studying me. "Wait a minute."

"What?" I had a premonition things were about to get tense.

"That reaction a minute ago," she said.

"What reaction?" I could stay cool, keep my face blank. At work I negotiated sales, rents, financing deals without giving away my angle to clients. So why did it seem like my new daughter-in-law could read my thoughts?

"Your reaction when I mentioned Avery."

I shrugged. "I was just surprised."

"Mmmhmm. It just so happens Avery texted me that he was spending the night, or part of it anyway, with a man, a hot older man."

Carter looked back and forth from me to her. "Wait. Are you calling my dad hot?"

She huffed. "Seriously, Carter. Look at him."

Now I was sure my face was as red as Carter's. "Felicity."

"He's gay, dear." She patted his hand. "So he's not a threat, and I think someone we know is already keeping him busy."

"You and Avery?" Carter said. The look of shock on his face would've been funny if he wasn't my son.

"Um…" Damn. I wasn't going to lie. I'd sworn I would never lie to Carter again.

Felicity laughed. "That sly bastard."

"Me or Avery?"

She just laughed.

"Were you going to say something or…" Carter was pale now instead of red.

"Are you okay?" Felicity asked him.

"I… Yeah." He grabbed his beer and drained the rest of it.

"If we decided to see each other again, I was going to tell you after the honeymoon, but Avery was afraid you'd be angry."

"Angry? No… But it's weird. I mean, you could be his dad."

"Or Avery could be your stepdad," Felicity said, smiling like a satisfied fox.

Carter sputtered, nearly choking on a fry. Then he simply dropped his head into his hands. I signaled our server and asked for another round of drinks.

"If Avery is worried about me, he shouldn't be," Felicity said. "I just want to see him happy."

Carter was potentially hyperventilating, and Felicity seemed to think Avery and I were going to keep seeing each other. But at least neither of them had run screaming or told me off.

"We're not sure this is going anywhere. He hasn't…" Shit, what did I say? I wasn't supposed to be talking to them about this at all.

"You want to see him again?" Felicity asked.

Carter groaned. "Are we really having this conversation? You do realize this is my dad, right?"

Felicity just waved him off.

"I would like to see him again, yes. I asked him to stay the weekend with me."

"Oh, wow," Carter squeaked. He still looked pale.

"I didn't seek this out."

He nodded, but Felicity raised her brows, clearly unconvinced.

"Honestly, he came to me."

"He's going to be in so much trouble when I get back," Felicity said.

"Please, don't give him too hard of a time. He's really nervous about how you'll react."

"Well, yeah," Carter said. "You're my dad and he's… Avery."

"I knew something was up when he was all coy about who he was with last night. He's usually not shy talking about his hookups. He scares poor Carter a bit."

Felicity patted his hand as she picked up the last of her burger.

"He's not going to talk about…" Carter gestured toward me with his beer glass.

I agreed. "No, that would be… Just no."

Felicity laughed. "You two are adorable. This almost makes up for our flight being cancelled."

"What? That's terrible. Did you get on another flight?"

Carter nodded. "We did, but it doesn't leave until tomorrow morning."

"So you'll be here another night?"

"Yeah. We couldn't keep the same room, but at least they had something open."

"I'm so sorry." And really hoping Avery and I didn't run into them.

Felicity shrugged. "It's okay. I love it here, and all that really matters is we're married."

Carter looked at her, his expression so lovestruck I was about to cry in the middle of a restaurant. I was also, very sadly, jealous.

I'd been playing around ever since my divorce. Sowing all the oats I didn't when I was younger. I'd told myself I didn't want anything serious, that I didn't need that. I thought I deserved to sleep with as many men as I could, and maybe that was true for a while. Maybe I did need that freedom, but for the last year or so, I'd known I was lying when I said I didn't need a relationship. I was ready to beg Avery to give me a chance. I wanted this to be more than a weekend, because while I'd played Daddy with some other boys, even kept them around for a few weeks or played regularly with them at Leo's club, I'd never felt a connection like this. I hadn't even realized how deep my feelings could go until Avery.

"Are you going to tell Avery you know about us?" I asked, looking at Felicity. I doubted Carter would say anything. He'd be too embarrassed.

She studied me for a few moments. "Not until I'm back, but I don't like him keeping this from me. We usually tell each other everything."

"I told him we should just confess, even if it didn't go any further."

Felicity huffed. "He's stubborn as fuck."

I supposed he was most of the time, but with me he was pliant, willing to surrender, even when he was unsure. "I'll try to convince him to call you."

Carter cleared his throat, and I looked his way. "Dad, I think you should tell Avery we guessed you were together, or Felicity did. I… Wow. I wouldn't have guessed. Do you usually go out with guys my age?"

Heat rushed to my face again. Damn, I hadn't blushed this much in years. "Sometimes. Not always." I'd gone out with several men my own age, but I was known at Leo's club for liking the Daddy/Dom vibe, so I usually had twinks chasing after me.

"Okay. I'm…" He paused for a breath. "It's going to take me a while to adjust, but I'm really glad you told me."

"You are?"

"Yes, because…" He paused to take a sip of his drink. "If you'd just talked to me before you left. If you'd explained…"

"You wished I'd come out to you, told you what I was going through."

He nodded. "You just left."

"Your mom…" She'd told me not to call him, but he was seventeen, almost an adult. I should have tried harder. "I'm sorry. I wish I had. I let your mom make decisions when I should have fought harder."

"It's okay now. But I do think you need to tell Avery everything. He deserves complete honesty."

I glanced at Felicity, but she held up her hand. "You have to decide that for yourself."

Carter was probably right, but Avery might feel betrayed. He might walk away when I needed more time to show him how good things could be between us.

Hasn't he seen that already? Doesn't he deserve to know?

"You're thinking awfully hard," Carter said.

I nodded. "I don't want to fuck this up."

"You really like him."

"From the moment I saw him." I'd even been intrigued by Carter's description.

"I can't believe you hadn't met before when you've been in Asheville," Carter said.

"That's my fault." Felicity had a sheepish look on her face.

"What do you mean?" I asked.

"You're completely his type, total catnip for him, and until I knew you a little better, I was worried about that. Now I'm not."

It took me a few seconds to process that. "You knew we'd be into each other."

"I thought you'd hook up. As to anything more… I wasn't sure. Avery doesn't usually…"

Carter gave her a pointed look.

"Sorry. I talk too much. Ignore me."

I didn't push, even though I wanted to. What was she going to say? Avery doesn't usually what, see a man more than once? Have real relationships? Obviously hooking up with older men was something he'd done before. How hard was I going to have to fight for him?

I wanted to ask, but I couldn't expect Felicity to spill her best friend's secrets.

I looked back at Carter. "Are you all right with this? Truly?" I wanted Avery desperately, but I wasn't going to risk ruining my relationship with my son.

His nose wrinkled like he was thinking hard, then he nodded. "Yeah. It's strange. Really strange. So I'm not going to think too hard about it, but if this becomes something more, then yeah, I'm okay with it."

"And Mandy and Wren, how do you think they'll feel?"

"I think they'll be fine," Carter said.

"Mandy will absolutely love it."

We both looked at Felicity.

"What? She'll think it's hilarious."

"Do I want to know why?" I asked.

Felicity grinned. "Avery's impossible. And she'll love what he'll put you through. She's also not as much of a prude as Carter."

"What? I'm not."

She stared at him.

"All right, fine. She's more comfortable than me with… sex things."

"Sex things?" Felicity mouthed to me.

I decided it was time to get out of there. I pushed back from the table and laid a hand on Carter's shoulder. "You think you'll recover?"

"Maybe, though I have a feeling this is basically what I've signed up for."

"That's sadly true." Felicity grinned, not seeming the least bit sorry.

"What time do you leave tomorrow?"

"We'll head to the airport around nine tomorrow morning," Carter said. "I'll send you the flight details."

"Thanks. Have a wonderful time. Call me when you're back and send some pictures of the beach."

"We will," Felicity assured me.

I hugged them both and then headed toward my suite, trying to make myself walk at a normal pace.

CHAPTER TEN

AVERY

I paced the room, hoping Felicity and Carter needed to eat quickly and get to the airport. I'd tried to ignore the plug in my ass. And I'd reminded myself that surely the remote couldn't work from as far away as the overlook restaurant. I'd driven to my apartment—that was uncomfortable as hell. Fortunately Sean wasn't there, so I didn't have to explain about my weekend. I grabbed some more clothes and a few toiletries. Then I came back to the hotel and ordered room service. I tried watching a movie as I ate, but every damn time I leaned over to pick up my sandwich, the plug shifted, and I had to fight the urge to pull out my cock and jerk myself off.

I couldn't decide what was more torturous, working my hips to let the plug rub me like I needed it to, or holding still, sweating as it pressed against me, making me want. It wasn't even that big. It shouldn't be so irritating, so hot, so just… there.

Would Graham make me wait even longer to come once he returned? Did some perverted part of me want him to? No. Yes. Ugh. I just needed him here.

What are you going to do in a few days? You'll be leaving, and he'll be going back to Charlotte. Then you won't have a Daddy anymore.

Was there a chance he really wanted more? He'd implied it, but I knew I shouldn't get my hopes up. I shouldn't be longing for him like this, not this soon. But what he did to me, not just the sex, but the way he made me feel needed and cherished, was incredible. I'd never really had that before.

My parents weren't monsters or anything, but they were both workaholics and rarely had time for me. When I told them I was gay, they didn't yell or kick me out, they just quietly made it clear that having a gay son was socially awkward. Once I left home, I only visited for holidays. They didn't seem to care that we rarely saw each other, so now, even though we lived fifteen miles apart, I rarely saw them. My sister, on the other hand, visited almost daily with her husband and her perfect children. They were all nice to me when I visited, coolly nice, like they would be to a stranger. It was weird and uncomfortable, and I'd spent last Christmas with Felicity and her mom.

Wouldn't it be nice if this year... No, Graham was a hot weekend fling. We weren't going to be more. I was certainly not going to be bringing him to Christmas dinner.

I heard someone in the hall and tensed. Could that be Graham? The door rattled as he pushed in the key. Thank God I wasn't going to have to wait any longer.

He stepped into the room, and I knelt. I didn't even think about it. The look on his face when he saw me transformed him from Graham to Daddy, and I simply knew what I needed to do.

"Have you been a good boy?"

"Yes, Daddy."

"Did you touch yourself?"

"No, Daddy."

"Hmm." He circled me, letting his fingers trail over one shoulder and then the other. I didn't know what he was looking for. What did he think would give me away if I were lying?

Finally he moved in front of me again. "I'm very proud of you, boy. Stand and strip and then stretch out on your back."

I'd expected him to turn on the vibrations to see if I could stay in position while he tormented my ass. I'd been scared I would fail him. But now, I was even more nervous because I wasn't sure what he wanted from me. I didn't think it would be as simple as getting me in bed and then getting me off.

He watched me intently as I removed my clothes. A few times he moved his hand toward his pocket, and I tensed, expecting him to go for the remote. He laughed at my jumpiness, the bastard.

You love the way he's teasing you.

I totally did.

"Daddy?"

"Yes, boy?"

"I… I'm not…" I chewed my lip, needing to confess how nervous I was and yet afraid to.

"I told you to tell me everything you're feeling. I will never be angry with my boy if he talks honestly to me." Graham got an odd look on his face then, one I couldn't read.

"I'm afraid I'll come if you touch me. I want to please you, but I don't know if I can."

"That's good, boy. Daddy is very proud of you for being honest. Eventually we'll work on you being able to hold off longer on your own."

Eventually? That word sent my heart racing, because it meant he did want to see me again. "Daddy, if you want me to, I'll try."

He shook his head. "I'm going to put a cock ring on you, because what I want is to pleasure you. Yes, I want to push your limits, but I don't want you so worried about coming too soon that you can't enjoy what we're doing."

"Thank you, Daddy. You're so good to me."

"That's because I want to make you happy. I want to give my boy what he needs."

I bit my lip to hold in a groan. It made me so hot for him to talk like that.

"Go lay on the bed. I'll get what we need."

"Yes, Daddy."

I stretched my arms over my head and spread my legs.

When Graham returned, he smiled. "You know exactly how I want you."

I loved how pleased he looked.

He held up a black satin sleep mask. "I'd like you to wear this. I want you to focus on what you feel. Is that okay with you?"

"Yes, Daddy." I knew I'd be safe with him, and with the mask on I wouldn't constantly be watching for him to reach for the remote. "I think it will make things easier for me."

"I think you're right, boy."

He put the blindfold in place, and I tried to relax, taking deep breaths and shifting until I was as comfortable as I could be when the damn plug in my ass jostled with even the smallest movement. I opened my legs more, and it bumped my prostate, making me gasp.

Graham laughed, and I was glad I had the blindfold on so I couldn't see his mocking expression.

"Do you need your hands tied?" he asked.

I licked my lips before answering. "Do you want to tie them?"

"Hmm." His low rumble flitted over me like a caress. I arched up, needing to get closer to him.

"I love how responsive you are." His praise warmed me, and I whimpered a little.

"No, I don't want to restrain you. I want you to hold on to the pillow until I tell you otherwise. Can you do that? If not, then ask me to tie you. I do eventually want to see you with rope around your wrists."

"Really?"

"Yes, baby."

"Y-you have rope with you?" My voice sounded far too high-pitched.

He chuckled. "No, but my belt would do. You'd look good in that too."

He cupped my neck and stroked my throat with his thumb. My breath hitched and precum dripped onto my stomach. Graham slid his hands over my chest, stopping to pinch my nipples, which made me squirm. The plug teased my ass, making me desperate to be fucked. I groaned.

"What seems to be the problem?"

"The plug. It's… I want it out."

"Do you?"

I wanted to see him, to read what was in his eyes. I took a few shaky breaths. I was so hard, so needy. But I wasn't sure of what I really wanted. "I don't know."

"What if I want it to stay in?"

"Then I want that too."

"Good boy." His tone was low and soothing. I sank into the mattress in relief that he'd taken the decision from me. Then he tapped the end of the plug, and I cried out, squeezing the pillow so hard I was surprised it didn't rip. The sensations seemed even stronger when I couldn't see. Fuck, he was going to kill me.

He turned the vibrations on before I recovered. I tried so hard not to move, but he teased my nipples and kept increasing the intensity until they were so strong, I couldn't fight it. I fucked the air as he sucked my nipples. When he wrapped a hand around my cock, I cried out. "Too much. Daddy, please. Please."

Everything stopped at once. The only sound in the room was my ragged breathing. I could feel him looming over me, but I wanted to see him. All I had to do was let go of the pillow and rip off the blindfold, but I wouldn't. I was a good boy.

"So beautiful," he said. He must have bent down, because I could feel his warm breath on my ear. "My beautiful boy."

"Daddy." The word came out like a plea, but I didn't know what I was asking for.

"Just a little more, boy. I know you can take it."

"For you, Daddy."

"That's right. For me."

I wasn't actually sure I could take much more. If it hadn't been for the cock ring, I would've come as soon as he'd touched me. I wanted to do this, though. I wanted to please him.

He switched the plug back on, turning the vibrations all the way up immediately. I cried out, writhing, fingers digging into the pillow. I didn't move my arms, though. It was as if I were truly restrained.

Graham kissed my neck, my chest, my abdomen. He lowered the vibration strength, and I tried to pull in more air.

"I'm going to suck you, boy. And you're going to stay still and take it."

The words were low and silky. I wanted to have misunderstood, because there was no way I could take that.

"Daddy?"

He stroked my side. "You can do this, boy. I know you can."

He didn't give me any more time to think about it. He took my cock deep, the tip pressing against the back of his throat. Then he worked his lips up and down.

I shook all over as I fought to keep my hips still. Beads of sweat rolled down my face. He took me all the way to the root, and I couldn't stand it. I fucked up into him. He grabbed my hips and shoved them down, pinning me in place. I fought him. I couldn't stop myself. Tears rolled from my eyes, wetting the face mask.

"Please, Daddy. Please don't."

He let me go, then turned off the plug, but my tears kept coming.

"Boy, are you okay?" His voice was low and gentle.

I tried to speak, but I couldn't. He took off the blindfold and wiped my tears away.

"I'm so proud of you. You're such a good boy."

"But I didn't stay still. I didn't—"

"Shhh. You tried your best, and you wanted to please me. That matters more than anything. I know how hard this is for you. Your cock is aching. You've been suffering for me all day, and that makes me so happy."

"It does?"

"Yes, baby. You're everything I want." He kissed me as he cupped my face, caressing my cheeks with his thumbs.

"I've never cried like this with anyone else. This never… It never mattered this much." I turned away, not wanting to see his reaction.

"Avery, please look at me." He used my name, which sent warmth through me. I did as he asked.

"This hasn't ever mattered so much to me either."

"Yeah?"

He nodded. "Can you take just a little more?"

Could I? I felt ready to come apart. "Maybe. I'll try."

"That's all I ask, boy." With those words we were back in our roles, and I was okay with that.

He moved between my legs and tugged on the plug. "Push out." I did, and he pulled it partway out, then squirted some lube on it. I thought he was going to fuck me with the plug, but instead he traced my stretched rim with his finger, rubbing, teasing. Then he slipped a finger into me alongside the plug.

"Oh, fuck. I… That…"

"You like that, don't you?"

"Yes, but… Oh, fuck, it hurts."

He moved his finger in and out very gently. "Someday, I'd like to put a dildo and my cock inside you."

"Yes." The word was out before I even thought about it.

He smiled as he pulled his finger from me. I gasped when he yanked the plug the rest of the way out. I felt so open, so empty. But he coated his hand with lube and pushed his fingers into me. All four of them.

"Burns. It burns, Daddy. So full. Fuck, I'm so full."

"I know, boy." He worked his fingers in and out, making slow, shallow strokes.

It hurt, but it felt so good. I needed to come. Needed this. More of this. "Don't stop. Please don't stop."

He twisted his arm, making his fingers rotate inside me. I groaned, lifting my hips, trying to get more.

"That is so fucking hot," he said. "We're definitely going to play more with stretching your ass."

"Yes, Daddy. I want that."

He chuckled. "I can see that you do. And I want to please my good boy."

I felt the sting of tears again. It was almost too much, to be cared for like this.

"Now touch yourself," he said.

I bit my lip, wanting to protest that I couldn't take his fingers in me and friction on my cock.

"Trust me to know what you can take, boy."

Those words were all I needed to know I could do it. I could do anything. "Yes, Daddy."

I let go of the pillow, flexing my hand to work out the cramps. Then I wrapped my fingers around my cock and stroked, slowly at first, but I could tell Daddy wanted more from me. I gripped myself more tightly and moved my hand up and down, faster and faster. My cock was begging for release. My balls were so full they felt like they might burst. But with each stroke, I moved further into a place where it was all just sensation, I was beyond hurting, beyond need. Everything was okay because Daddy was there, encouraging me.

Daddy pulled his hand from my ass, and I cried out, but then he was stretched over me, his cock lined up with mine. He pushed my hand away and took us both in his hand, working us with a firm grip.

"So good. So good. Daddy. Need you, Daddy."

"I know, boy." He reached down and released the ring. I screamed as heat coiled in me. One stroke and I was shooting, crying out because it hurt and yet it was perfect, exquisite pleasure. Daddy came moments after me, his cum landing on top of mine, making me a sticky mess. I loved that feeling, loved being marked by him.

I ran my fingers through our mingled spunk and then licked them clean. Daddy made a low, growly noise.

"Do that again."

I did. And then he used his fingers to feed me more. "Enough," he said, when I was only partially cleaned up. "My cock can't take anymore, not right now."

I grinned at him. "Did I wear you out, Daddy?"

He scowled at me. "I'll wear your ass out."

"Please."

He lifted his brows and I giggled. "Okay, maybe not right now."

"That's what I thought, boy. We're going to shower, and then it will be time for our spa appointments."

"They had a slot for me?" I asked, sounding more eager than I'd meant to. I still felt a bit odd about him paying for a spa day for me.

"They'd had a cancellation, so your appointment starts just fifteen minutes after mine. After our massages, we can meet at the hot and cold pools."

"I don't suppose these are private pools."

He laughed. "They're not. But you should be able to restrain yourself for a few hours. What does it take to wear you out, boy?"

"I'm hoping we'll find out tonight."

He rolled his eyes. "Maybe I really am too old for this."

I sat up and laid a hand on his shoulder. "No, Daddy. You're perfect."

He grinned. "Come on. It's time for me to get my boy all cleaned up."

CHAPTER ELEVEN

AVERY

I didn't think I'd ever felt as relaxed as I did after my massage. I'd had massages before, but I'd never had a therapist as skilled as this one. I'd also never been fucked into oblivion right before my appointment and then lovingly washed like I was a prince with a very dedicated servant/lover. Not that I thought Graham was fantasizing about me being a prince as he worked me over with the world's softest sponge, but it was sure as hell what was in my mind.

I groaned as I slid my arms into the plush robe the therapist had laid out for me. She'd told me to take my time coming back to reality, not that my life felt very real at that moment. The rest of my afternoon was going to be spent taking in the pools and salt room with Graham. That was pretty damn far from my day-to-day reality. I drank the water my therapist had left me as I walked to the locker room and marveled at how loose I felt. I hadn't even realized how much tension I'd been holding in my shoulders. I really needed to find a way to thank Graham for this, a very dirty way to thank him.

I slipped off my robe and slid on my swim trunks, rainbow ones because why not be obvious. Then I checked the mirror to see how much of a mess my hair was. I repaired it as best I could with the gel I'd brought. Yes, I was sure you weren't supposed to worry about your hair in the spa, but I had a hot Daddy waiting for me, and I wanted him to thirst for me when I walked in.

I closed up my locker and wound my way around to find the door leading to the hot pool. Graham had texted me that he was soaking while he waited for me. When I stepped out into the pool room, I gasped. I'd heard great things about this spa, but I'd yet to indulge myself. Now that the tourism industry had taken off in a crazy way, day passes were getting harder to come by if you weren't a hotel guest.

The pools were underground, so the walls were made of rock. I felt like I was in some kind of tropical cave. Steam rose from the pool, and my skin was instantly damp, though the walls radiated coolness. I scanned the edge of the pool until I saw Graham. Damn, he looked fine. He turned as if he'd felt me staring, and I got exactly the reaction I wanted. His gaze fixed on me, and he watched every step I took as I descended the steps into the oh-my-God-that's-hot water. I moved toward him, my cock taking interest as I studied his broad chest and well-defined arms. I wanted to sink underwater and see if I could hold my breath long enough to suck him; unfortunately there were other people around, a few of whom I recognized from the wedding, so we had to keep things casual.

I settled next to him on the bench that circled the pool's edge.

"Enjoy your massage?" he asked.

I groaned, and his eyes narrowed.

"Less of the sex noises if you want to keep our relationship secret."

I laughed.

"So it was that good, huh?"

"It really was. The best one I've ever had. Thank you again for… everything."

He took my hand under the water and squeezed. "I couldn't be happier to give this to you."

"I just hope you have more to give me after we enjoy this place." I smirked at him, and he splashed me.

"Keep that up, and I'll find us a place to have more right now."

"You wouldn't." I let my mouth drop open in mock horror.

"Don't fucking tempt me."

"I'll do my best," I said, though part of me wanted to see if he really would drag me somewhere semi-private and fuck the hell out of me. "I can't stop wanting it around you."

"Me either. I haven't been this horny since I was your age."

I snickered. "Seriously?"

"Yes."

His tone told me he was telling the truth. I pulled my hand away and shifted so I could look at him. "This weekend… It's…"

"I want to see you again."

"You do?"

He nodded.

"But what about Carter?"

He looked away, and that was definitely not good. "What?"

"Nothing. I… I need to tell him, and you need to tell Felicity."

"Yeah. If we're going to see each other again, then we do."

He looked relieved.

"After the honeymoon?" I asked.

He nodded. "Right after."

"Okay." I wished I knew what Felicity would think. I could usually predict her reactions flawlessly, but I had no idea what she'd say about this. If Graham were anyone else, she'd be thrilled I'd found someone I wanted for more than a night of hot fucking, but he was her father-in-law now, and that was… weird didn't quite cover it. "Can we talk about something else now?"

"Yeah. You're supposed to be relaxing, but I can see you tensing up again."

I took a deep breath and let it out slowly, doing my best to shake off my anxiety.

"Turn around," Graham ordered.

"What?"

"Turn around. I'm going to calm you down."

"Here?" I squeaked.

"Yes, boy." I couldn't resist that commanding tone.

He slid his hands up and down my back. If one of the guests who knew us walked in… No, I wasn't going to think about that. I closed my eyes and surrendered to him. Daddy would take care of it.

By the time he stopped massaging me, I was back to that floaty place I'd been in after he'd fucked me. "You're good at this."

"Rubbing your back?"

"Being a Daddy, taking care of me."

He looked more uncertain than I'd seen him before. "You mean that?"

I cupped his face, still oblivious to anyone around us. "I do. I don't know how this happened, but I need you."

He smiled, looking more settled now. "I know."

"Not just your cock, you. Everything." Holy shit, had I really said that?

He held my gaze and suddenly the heat of the pool was too much. The room spun around me. "Um… I think I need…"

"The cold pool." He stood and pulled me out of the water.

"Can you walk?"

"I'm not sure." I was dizzy, and my dick was so hard.

He scooped me up with no hesitation. I heard a woman gasp, but I closed my eyes and tucked my head against his shoulder.

"Oh my!" a woman said. I couldn't tell if she was intrigued or shocked.

"He's overheated." Graham's voice brooked no contradiction.

"Well, I guess he would be," another woman said.

Someone else giggled.

I smiled against Graham's shoulder and whispered, "You'd overheat anyone."

He lowered me to the edge of the cold pool. "Put your feet in."

I shrieked. "Cold. Jesus, that's cold."

"That is the idea." He hopped off the side, plunging all the way in. After he surfaced and dragged in a few breaths, he grabbed me and pulled me under.

I squealed, and I was sure everyone was staring.

"We're going to get kicked out," I protested when I'd recovered from the shock.

He tugged me to the side, and we sat on the edge, me shivering with his arm around me. "No, we're not. I'll behave now."

I raised my brows. "Are you sure about that?"

He winked at me. "Hell, no."

"Can we try the salt room now? This is way too cold."

"Sure. Let's go."

I walked this time, and we didn't even touch. Maybe we could be good. I was determined we were just going to talk for a while, so I sat far enough from him that I wouldn't be tempted to run my hand along his muscular thighs, or through the damp hair on his chest, or… "Pretend you could go to any restaurant in the world. Where would it be and what would you eat?"

He looked slightly uncomfortable.

"Wait. You could like actually do that, couldn't you?"

"Maybe not anywhere and not any time but… yeah, I could."

I realized it wasn't that big of a deal to him to give me a spa day. "Wow."

He smiled and scooted closer, running his fingers along my arm. So much for being good.

"I want to take you everywhere."

I wasn't sure how to respond to that. "Um…"

"Shhh. We'll talk about that later. Let me think about your question."

I watched as he pondered, barely resisting the urge to run my finger along his cheek which was already stubbly despite him shaving that morning. How hot would he look with a salt-and-pepper beard? Fuck, he'd be delicious.

"All right." His voice startled me. I'd gotten lost in thoughts of his imaginary beard rubbing me as he ate my ass. "I would go to an amazing restaurant a friend recommended on the Kintyre peninsula in Scotland. He said they have the most amazing mussels and scallops he's ever eaten."

"Mmm. That sounds amazing."

"You like seafood?"

"Yeah, totally."

"Good. After dinner, we'd go back to a little cottage. There'd be a heated sunroom facing the sea. I'd take you out there and—"

"Any more, and I won't be able to sit still. We're supposed to be talking."

"I was."

"About sex," I protested.

"How do you know what I was going to say? I might have been going to serve you coffee or—"

I glared at him.

"Fine. Now it's your turn. What's your fantasy dinner?"

I frowned. "I don't know. There are so many places I want to go."

"Pick one."

I shivered. "Damn, I love it when you tell me what to do."

"Dinner."

He was way too good at this. "Well, this one is kinda cheesy compared to yours. I mean, it's such a thing that would be in the top ten international vacation destinations."

"Tell me."

"Tuscany. I want to go eat at a villa in Tuscany that's like on a farm where you have family-style dinner al fresco. Everything would be fresh, and the table would be covered in white linen even though you're outside. Dinner would last for hours. There would be wine and—"

"I know exactly the place to take you."

"What? Those places seriously exist?"

"Of course they do. I went on a farm-to-table tour in Tuscany with a friend a few years ago."

"A friend?"

"Yes. He was the first friend I made when I moved to Charlotte after the divorce. We were lovers briefly, but we make much better friends. I had a chance to travel, and I wanted someone with me who would enjoy it like I would and wouldn't complicate things."

"That sounds amazing."

"It was. Avery, I…"

I shook my head. I couldn't talk about us traveling together, not when we'd been together one night. My stomach rumbled, and I glanced toward the complimentary snack bar which was just through the doors at the outdoor pool.

"Hungry?" he asked.

"I guess that's a hazard of talking about fantasy dinners."

He rose from his chair, and I stared as water droplets ran down his chest, catching at the waist of his swim trunks. I wanted to lick them up.

"Grab us a table and I'll get something to eat."

I settled under an umbrella, and he joined me a few moments later with two glasses of prosecco and a plate full of fruit, olives, cheese, and crackers. I reached for a strawberry, but he swatted my hand away.

Before I could protest, he plucked it from the plate and held it up to my mouth. "I want to feed my boy."

Holy fuck. I bit into the strawberry, then licked the juice from his fingers.

He held my gaze as he handed me a glass. I took a sip of prosecco, then slowly licked my lips. Next he fed me an olive. This time I pulled one of his fingers into my mouth, sucking the salty brine from it and then enjoying the taste of his skin.

"I thought we were going to talk," he said when he pulled the digit from my mouth.

"We were, but you… you…"

"Am I distracting you?"

I rolled my eyes. "Oh, no, not at all. How would it be distracting to be fed by you?"

"I like taking care of you."

"I like it too. I never thought I'd find…" I glanced away, my eyes starting to burn.

"It's okay. We can just talk," he said.

I nodded.

"Tell me some of your favorite movies."

I wanted to thank him for saving me from crying again, but I was afraid the tears would come back if I tried. "You'll laugh at my choices."

"I doubt that."

"*Bridget Jones*. *Notting Hill*. Most rom-coms, really, but they get extra points if they're British. What about you?" I asked, not wanting to give him time to mock me.

"Um…" He glanced away toward the outside pool.

"Come on. They can't be worse than mine."

He sighed. "Not worse, more like the same."

My mouth dropped open. "Are you fucking with me?"

"What? No."

"So you seriously like *Bridget Jones*? Oh my God!"

"Shhh." He glanced around, face turning red.

"You don't mind people watching you carry me around, but you won't admit to liking romantic movies?" I practically shouted the last words, and he winced.

I couldn't help but laugh.

"It's one of my biggest secrets."

"Then you're going to have to tell me more because this one is delicious."

He sighed. "Frappuccinos. I love them."

"We are so getting some and watching a rom-com tonight."

He let his gaze slide over me. "That is not what I had planned for us."

I shivered. "Okay then, tomorrow."

"Maybe."

"Tell me more."

He shook his head. "Not until you spill something embarrassing."

I pondered. What could I reveal to him that wouldn't completely kill me? "At fourteen, I jerked off thinking of Justin Timberlake at least once a day."

"No fucking way. Seriously?"

I covered my face. "Yes."

"What else?"

"I have to tell more?"

"If you want more from me, you do."

"I've seen every episode of *House Hunters International*."

He shrugged. "That's not so bad."

"Hold up. Do you like it too?"

He studied the underside of our umbrella. "I have no idea what you're talking about."

"You really are perfect, aren't you?"

He turned even redder than he had when I'd yelled that he liked rom-coms. "I have plenty of faults."

"Me too, but I… I still…"

He took my hand and squeezed. "It's okay. Why don't you tell me how you ended up working at the salon?"

Shit. He'd had to save me once again from getting too sentimental. It was like he'd turned me to fucking mush.

You're falling for this man.

No. No way, he was just… we had good chemistry and similar kinks and oh God, he really was fucking perfect.

"When I graduated from high school, I had no idea what I wanted to do. I was happy just to have survived and to be able to start being myself a little more freely. My parents were willing to pay for college. Felicity was leaving me to go to Duke, and I didn't have a good job lined up, so I figured what the hell. Even though I didn't know what I wanted to do, I went to UNC-Asheville. I met Sean, who's my roommate now. He was working at the salon on the weekends while he got his degree. I told him I loved doing my friends' hair and makeup, so he brought me to work with him one day. I ended up talking to his manager during lunch. He loved the ideas I had, but I needed to be certified to work there as a stylist. I was disappointed, but I kept taking classes toward a degree in sociology."

"What were you planning to do with it?"

"I'd thought about working as a counselor at a health clinic. I wanted to do something to help people."

He nodded. "I can see that."

"So summer came, and I needed a job. The receptionist at the salon had just quit, so they hired me.

The more I worked there, the more I knew that was what I wanted to do. I quit UNC-A and got certified in cosmetology so I could start working as a stylist. I've been there ever since."

"So Sean still works there, too, and he's your roommate?"

Was that a hint of jealousy in his voice? I smiled. "After he got his degree, he found a job as a technical writer. And yes, he's my roommate, but that's all. Trust me, we would be a disaster as a couple. We've fucked for stress relief a few times, but we both prefer bottoming and our craziness feeds off each other. We both need someone to keep us in line."

"I could keep you in line."

"Mmm, you sure could, Daddy."

He glanced toward the edge of the patio. "What?"

"I'm considering how well those trees would cover us if I dragged you over there for a blowjob."

I made a choking sound. "Talking. We're supposed to be talking."

"Right."

"What about you? How did you become a real estate mogul?"

He rolled his eyes. "I worked for a development company. They weren't doing great. I had some ideas on how to improve things. They worked. I moved up in the ranks and eventually bought them out. After my divorce, I expanded and opened an office in Charlotte."

"Damn."

He shrugged. "My grandmother passed away. She'd invested well. I used the money to make a gamble."

"A good one, apparently."

He nodded. "I'm doing quite well for myself, but you haven't landed a billionaire or anything."

I glanced at my phone. "Oh, no. Look at the time. I'd better—"

He laid a hand on my thigh and dug his fingers in. "Boy, you're not going anywhere."

I shivered, loving his dominance. "No, Daddy. I'm not."

We watched each other for a moment. I wondered if he would kiss me. I didn't even care who might be looking. If I had to be waiting for Felicity at the airport when she came back so I could be the first one to tell her, that's what I would do.

"Do you see yourself staying here, working at the salon?"

I nodded. "For now, anyway. Not necessarily forever. I love Asheville, but it's getting more expensive and more crowded every year."

"You're happy though? You truly love what you do?"

"Yeah, I am. I have a job I enjoy. Friends. I live in a gorgeous city." And now I had the possibility of something special with a crazy hot man. "What about you?"

He seemed to consider his answer for a few moments. "I enjoy my job, especially when I can seek new challenges, but sometimes, I feel like something's missing. Or I did."

He looked apprehensive, so I reached for his hand. "You... did?"

"For the first year or two after I came out, I was one of the biggest sluts at my friend's club."

"Wow. That, um... Wow."

He rolled his eyes. "So cliché, huh? Letting loose after years in the closet."

"It is, but it's become cliché for a reason."

"True. For a while now I've known I wanted something more. Something deeper. I told you I'd played Daddy and boy before, but it's never been more than that—play. With you, I can imagine it being more than just a game. Not that I want to do it twenty-four seven, but…"

"I've wanted someone to take care of me for years. I told myself it was stupid. That I just felt that way because my parents were shit or because I was too immature to be a real grown-up."

"You seem to be doing just fine supporting yourself."

"I am. I'm not set for life like you, but I have a nice apartment, a good job."

"And you're damn good at what you do."

I smiled. "Thanks. I would like to have my own makeup line one day."

"You would?"

I was a little nervous to admit this. I'd only told a few people, but somehow I knew he wouldn't laugh. "I've started making some products. Right now, I'm just playing around, but I'd love to keep developing them."

"You need to keep working on it. I want to see what you can do."

I felt warm all over at his obvious excitement. "So you really think this—us—could be more?"

He shifted and looked away like he was nervous, which made me want to comfort him. I took his hand in mine and stroked the back of it with my thumb. He lifted his eyes, meeting my gaze. "Yes."

"Okay. Me too." If he could be vulnerable, so could I.

He exhaled slowly. "I'd love to extend this trip, but I just can't. I can come back in two weeks, though."

"Really?"

He nodded.

"I usually work Saturdays but I'm off Sundays and Mondays. I know that's probably not good for your schedule."

"I've hardly taken any time off in the last two years. I can take a Monday or more. In fact, with a little juggling, I can do some work remotely and take a full week. It is my company, after all."

"Yeah, I guess it is."

He turned my hand over and traced patterns on my palm. "So that's okay with you? For me to come back?"

"It's more than okay." The words came out all breathless; his simple touch was sending shivers up my arm. I was in danger of getting a hard-on that everyone would see.

Heat flashed in his eyes. "Next time I'll bring more toys for us to try out."

Now all I could think about was the remote-controlled plug. "Should I be excited or nervous?"

"Both." His lips curled in an evil smile. "Definitely both."

"I think I need the cold pool again."

He grinned. "Let's go."

CHAPTER TWELVE

GRAHAM

Avery and I spent another hour or so enjoying the pool and the sauna. Then we showered, not together, despite me trying to convince him it was our duty to conserve water, and dressed. The elevator from the spa only went to the main floor. So we had to exit and walk down the hall to go up to my suite.

When we stepped out of the car, I was holding Avery's hand. I couldn't resist touching him every chance I got. He made me so fucking happy, and I didn't know how I was going to stand being in Charlotte for two weeks without him.

Then we turned into the corridor and Avery froze, making me stumble.

He jerked his hand away from me. "Shit."

Carter and Felicity were walking toward us. Time seemed to slow, giving me far more than a few seconds to regret not telling Avery what had happened at lunch. Why the fuck had I sat there talking about telling them as if they didn't know? If he figured out I'd deceived him, he wouldn't want to see me again. I did not want to fucking lose him.

"We can just pretend we met up at the spa," Avery said.

"We were holding hands."

"They probably didn't see." They might not have if he hadn't jerked away, but he'd made it pretty obvious.

"Avery, listen, I should have—"

"Hey y'all! What are you up to?" Felicity called.

It was too late for me to confess, and she was acting as if it were perfectly normal to see us together. I stared, trying to silently beg her to pretend not to know.

"I thought you'd left already," Avery said.

"Our flight got cancelled, didn't Dad tell you?" Carter asked.

"No." Avery glanced over at me.

I forced a smile. "Sorry. I got distracted."

Avery seemed to accept that answer.

"So did you two like go to the pool together or something?"

Thank you, Carter. At least he was pretending to be surprised.

"Sort of," Avery said. "We, um… We met at the spa, actually."

Carter frowned at him. "I thought you were headed home last night."

Felicity, on the other hand, was giving us a knowing look.

"I didn't get a room," Avery said. "But I had the day off, so I thought why not get a spa pass."

Carter nodded. "The spa's great, isn't it? We went last week. Felicity said I had to try it."

"Oh, yeah, she loves it."

Avery's voice sounded off, and I realized he was giving Felicity an odd look, but Carter asked me about the nature reserves I'd visited when I was in Trinidad, and I had to pay attention to him.

When I'd listed off a few suggestions, I glanced over at Felicity and Avery. It was like one of those moments in a dream when you know something's about to happen and you want to stop it, but you're rooted to the spot with your mouth sealed closed.

"I can't believe you aren't teasing about this." Felicity looked away.

Say something, I screamed in my mind. *Tease him about being with me. Make an inappropriate joke. Something.*

"I just thought… Um…" Who would've thought Carter would be the better actor of the pair? He clearly needed to give Felicity some lessons.

"Felicity," Carter said, a warning in his voice. She didn't acknowledge him.

"Thanks for trying," I whispered. I was doomed. And it was my own fault.

"Oh, God. You know, don't you?" Avery said. Felicity winced and nodded.

"How? Did you see us last night, or…" He glanced at me. "Oh shit, he told you."

"No, it wasn't like that." Surprisingly, it was Carter who spoke.

"I can't believe it." Avery took a step away from me.

"Please just listen. I—"

"We talked about telling them, and you acted like they didn't know." His tone was vicious. I could see the hurt and anger in his eyes.

"Avery, I—"

He shook his head. "Don't. This was all a mistake." He turned and fled, racing through the lobby and pushing past a family who was coming in the main entrance.

I started after him, but Felicity grabbed my arm. "Let him go. He needs a chance to cool down."

"I don't think he has his keys or his wallet, and he shouldn't drive like this anyway."

"What about his phone?" Felicity asked.

I thought for a second. "Yes, he's got it." He'd taken a picture of us in the plush waiting room of the spa before we'd left, saying he needed something to help him remember one of the best days of his life. A day I'd now ruined.

I squeezed my eyes shut. Once again, I'd fucked up, because I was too afraid to be completely honest with someone I cared about. "You were right, Carter. I should have listened to you."

"Yeah, I really hoped you would."

"Next time you give me advice, remind me what happens when I ignore you."

Felicity laid a hand on my arm. "I feel like this is all my fault. I shouldn't have said anything yesterday. I should've just let you have your secret."

"No, this is not on you. Avery was nervous about telling you, and I didn't want to ruin the magic of this weekend, so I kept it from him."

"Magic?" Carter sounded pained.

Felicity gave his arm a light slap. "Romantic magic. Don't you get it?"

He frowned. "Get what?"

"You dad's in love with Avery."

"In love?" Carter sounded like he was choking.

"Did you really think this was about fucking? They would've had the sense to be more discreet then. Graham would probably have just sent him home afterward."

"But… But… They just met yesterday."

108

I stood there openmouthed as they talked about me. I honestly had no idea how to respond. In love with Avery? No way was I in love with him. Not yet…

"How long did it take you to know?" Felicity asked Carter. "With me."

Carter frowned. "I knew the moment I saw you, but—"

"Exactly. I was stubborn, so it took me a while to admit how I felt. But no matter what I told you or myself, I knew you were the right one for me all along."

"Really?" The look of joy on his face made me smile despite my fear Avery was gone for good.

"Yes." She turned to me then. "I'm going after Avery. He'll either walk around a bit or call his roommate to come get him."

"His bag is in my suite."

"Then he'll have to come back for it," she declared.

"No. I want you to take it to him. I don't want him to think I'm trying to trap him into coming back. If he doesn't want to see me again, that's his choice."

Felicity's lips curved up. "That just won you a hell of a lot of points."

"I wasn't trying to—"

"I know." She turned to Carter. "You stay here in case Avery comes back. I'll run up with your dad and get Avery's stuff. Then if he hasn't returned, I'll track him down."

Felicity took my arm and we started walking toward the elevator. "Unlock your phone and give it to me."

I was basically on autopilot, so I did what she told me.

When we reached the elevator, she handed it back. "I put Avery's number in. Text him. Apologize again, then tell him I guessed, and you didn't want to lie."

I told myself he wasn't going to respond, but when he hadn't by the time we reached my suite, I couldn't help feeling even more hopeless.

"Gather up his stuff, and if he hasn't texted you back when I leave, call him."

"I'm not sure he'll—"

"Trust me. I've known him most of his life. He may not answer, but he'll like knowing you're thinking about him."

I put Avery's makeup bag back into his duffel and looked around for anything else he hadn't already packed up. "I think his tux is the only other thing. I can return it for him."

She nodded. "All right, but don't assume you'll have to. I'm betting he'll be back and can get it himself."

"I wish I had your confidence."

"He tends to panic and overreact. Then he regrets it and wishes he'd talked things through. Just give him some time."

"All right. I'll be right here until I have to check out on Monday morning."

"I have your number, so I'll text you after I talk to him, okay?"

"You shouldn't be doing this now. You're supposed to be on your honeymoon." I hadn't even thought of that until now. I was being so fucking selfish.

"Carter and I are both antsy waiting to get going. There's only so much time you can spend in your room before you get—"

"Nothing TMI, please."

She laughed. "Let me do this for you. I know what you said, but I still feel like it's my fault."

I hugged her tightly. "Thank you."

"Don't give up, okay?"

"Okay."

After she left, I flopped on the couch and pulled out my phone. No texts. I called Avery, but it went to voicemail. I left a pathetic message. Then I paced the length of my suite. I had a feeling it was going to be a really long evening.

CHAPTER THIRTEEN

AVERY

I was curled up on the couch in my apartment. So far I'd refused Sean's offers of water, coffee, and vodka. I was too numb to cry, too devastated to talk, and angry at myself for all of it. I'd wanted to fuck a hot guy, that was all. I'd never meant to feel what I did, and now everything was fucked up. Why had Graham lied? He could have just told me.

And have you freak out?

Fine. Maybe I should have ignored Felicity's odd reaction. If I hadn't known her so well, I wouldn't have even thought about it. But there was no way she didn't think Graham would push all my buttons—and did he ever, more than Felicity even realized. I'd never told her my Daddy kink went quite as far as it did. I hadn't even really known that myself.

If I'd just ignored that little voice saying something wasn't right, I could've stumbled through my fake story of why I was with Graham. Then after the honeymoon, I would've overanalyzed what to say to her, practiced my speech, and prayed Felicity and Carter would be okay with it.

Instead, I find out they already know and apparently… They're. Fine. With. It.

Fuck. They're fine with it. They don't care. There's nothing to stress about.

"But Graham kept it from me." I said the last words out loud.

Sean patted my hand as he sat down on the coffee table, ignoring that there were actual chairs available. "Yes, baby, he did, but he's called how many times?"

I sighed and glanced at my phone. "Four."

"And texted…?"

I shook my head. "I can't look."

"Because you might read them?"

I nodded. "And because… he's probably…"

"Hurting too?"

I glared at him. "Are you taking his side?"

Sean shook his head. "I'm saying that if it was just a hookup for him, if he didn't care, he wouldn't pursue you. From what you told me, he could easily find someone else to fuck."

The thought of Graham calling someone else "boy" made my chest ache. I curled into an even tighter ball.

"You don't like that, do you?"

I slid my hand out from the blanket I'd pulled over myself and flipped him off. "Fuck you."

Someone knocked on the door, and Sean hopped up.

"Wait. What if it's—"

Sean ignored me, opening the door without even checking.

Felicity stormed in and dropped my bag on the floor. "I guessed, you asshole. Graham didn't tell us. I guessed, and he thought you'd be upset that he hadn't managed to lie to me."

"No one can lie to you," Sean said, looking awed.

He was right. Felicity was like a tornado. It was best to just get out of her way.

"I think he's in love with you," she said.

"In… what?" I sputtered. I couldn't seem to get air into my lungs.

Sean snorted. "I think you broke him."

"Oh hush." She waved a hand at him. "He knew. He just didn't want to think about it."

"He's… And I… Oh, fuck. What is happening?" I decided she had, in fact, broken me.

"You ran off without giving Graham or me a chance to talk. That's what happened."

Sean whistled. "Damn, she just tells it like it is."

Felicity glared at him.

"At the spa Graham and I talked about telling you after your honeymoon, and he never… he just sat there and let me make plans."

She nodded. "I'm not saying that was right, but I do believe he thought he was doing the right thing. Stupid as that may be."

"It's… I just… I have to be able to trust him, if we…"

"If you what?"

"If we're going to be more than a hookup." And if he's going to be my Daddy who can take care of me by fucking me until I let go and sob.

"I'm pretty sure you're falling in love too," Sean said.

I groaned. "Why are you so perceptive?"

"It's not like it's hard to see. You were crying when you called me, and you've been acting like you're dying since I got you home."

I sniffed. "Sometimes I wish I had normal friends."

Felicity raised her brows. "Normal?"

"Ones that didn't notice things."

"No, you don't," Sean said, sitting on the coffee table again and petting my head.

"You're going back over there right now," Felicity said.

"No! I can't. I ran away. I didn't even have my keys or my stuff. I just walked off and didn't say anything. I didn't even look at him." I dropped my head into my hands, wishing the couch would consume me.

"He said he wouldn't leave the hotel until he has to check out in case you came back. Trust me. He wants to see you."

I looked up at Felicity. "He really said that?"

She nodded.

Sean was staring at me. "What did you do to this Daddy?"

Heat rushed to my face. "Um… things. Good things."

Felicity grimaced. "That's my father-in-law we're talking about."

"Yeah, but didn't you say yourself that he was hot?" Sean asked.

"Yes, but it's still gross to think about him fucking Avery."

"Can you both just stop?" I begged.

Felicity ignored me, continuing to focus on Sean. "Gross as it is, if it bothers Avery enough to make him leave, then I guess I'll have to keep doing it." She looked at me then. "The daddy thing really does it for you, huh?"

"Seriously, shut up." If only she knew. Really knew. I could feel my face getting redder.

"Are you ready to go back to the hotel? Because if not, I will keep going, and none of us want that."

"I'm okay with it, actually," Sean said.

We both looked at him, and he held up his hands. "I'm a pervert, okay?"

Based on the plug with a horse's tail I'd accidentally found when looking for some jeans he'd borrowed, he damn well was. Not that I minded.

"Just go talk to him," Sean said. "Even if you're still mad."

"I don't even know what I'm feeling. I was startled and angry and hurt, and then I was embarrassed that I ran."

"You can tell him all those things," Felicity said. "Even if you don't want to see him again, you at least need to go talk this through."

I didn't say anything for a few moments as I tried to sort through my emotions. Finally, I came to a conclusion. "I still want him."

Felicity smiled. "I thought so."

"But I—"

Sean sighed. "Stop analyzing and just go get him."

"So I just walk in there and—"

"Knock first," Sean said. "If he's really missing you, then he might be…" Sean mimed jacking off.

"Oh. My. God." Felicity pressed her hand against her eyes as if trying to block out that image.

"You said we should keep talking about it if he didn't go, and he hasn't—"

"Sean. Stop being gross," Felicity screeched.

I ran for the door. When I got there, I realized my car keys were at the hotel along with my car. "Um… Can someone give me a ride?"

Felicity grabbed her purse. "I'm heading back that way, but no sex talk in the car."

Sean sighed. "Poor Carter, married to a prude."

"Sean, you are walking a thin line. If I wasn't a happy blushing bride I might have to stab you."

Sean laid a hand over his heart. "Whew! Lucky me."

"Come on." I tugged on Felicity's arm.

I was so nervous on the drive there I hardly said anything. When we parked, Felicity squeezed my hand. "You'll be fine. Just stay calm, tell him why you were so hurt, and—"

"I don't want to have to talk."

Her eyes narrowed. "Do not try to cover this up with sex."

"I wouldn't—"

"Avery, I know you."

I huffed. "Fine. No sex before I talk to him."

"Good. Now go."

I did.

CHAPTER FOURTEEN

GRAHAM

Someone knocked on my door and my pulse sped up. It was probably housekeeping. But what if... I held my breath as I looked through the peephole.

Avery stood there, chewing on his lip.

I yanked the door open, startling him. He was pale. His face tearstained. "I'm sorry. Really sorry."

"Me too. For running. I'm not good with confrontation."

"And I'm not good at knowing when to admit things I'd rather hide."

Avery glanced down at his feet and nodded. I realized then that we were still in the doorway. "Come in, please."

He did.

I reached out to lay a hand on his back but pulled away before making contact. As much as I wanted to touch him, I knew we needed to talk things through first.

When we were both seated on the sofa, I said, "I should have told you right away. I was afraid you'd be angry or upset, and I was selfish because I wanted the time with you. I didn't want you to leave, but keeping it from you made you leave anyway."

"I came back." His voice was shaking, and I would have done anything to make him happy again.

"Why?" I needed to know, even if the answer wasn't what I was hoping for.

"Felicity told me she guessed I'd spent the night with you. She said you only reluctantly admitted it. I was upset because no one's ever taken care of me like you have this weekend. I couldn't reconcile you knowing exactly what I needed and then deceiving me. It hurt. A lot."

I started to speak, but he held up his hand.

"Felicity truly believes you meant well. If she trusts you, then maybe I still can."

I still had a chance. *Don't screw this up.* "I did mean well. It was stupid, but I thought I was taking care of you by not saying anything. But I shouldn't keep things from you. Doing what's best for you means comforting you if you're upset, not trying to keep you from hearing something upsetting."

"That's… You're amazing."

He reached for my hand, and I twined my fingers with his. "I'm not. I'm an idiot a lot of the time, but I can learn."

"I think I can too. I should've stayed and listened, but I panicked. I'm sorry for that."

"You don't need to—"

"Just listen. Please. I was so happy, and then I thought maybe I couldn't trust you after all, which meant we couldn't play the games we liked, and I would lose you and—"

I cupped his face and made him look at me. "Avery, we don't have to play any games for me to want you. I love being your Daddy, but I still want you no matter what we do in bed."

"Y-you do?"

I slid from the couch and dropped to my knees. "I do. Please forgive me."

His eyes watered, then tears spilled over, and it was all I could do not to cry too.

"I forgive you." He stood and tugged on my hands to pull me to my feet.

I brushed the back of my hand over his cheek. "I want to kiss you."

"Yes, I want that too."

I leaned down, but stopped before our lips touched. "I don't know how this happened. Maybe I've gone crazy, but being with you just feels so right. I want to play Daddy and boy with you, but I also just want to hold you close and see what can happen between us."

"Me too. That's really why I ran. I wanted this so much, and then I thought I'd misjudged you and it was all going to fall apart. I should have stayed and listened to you."

"No, I should've been honest from the start."

He smiled. "Next time you will be."

"I will. I promise." I kissed him then. He opened to me, and I felt him surrender. I held his hips tightly, pulling him close so I could grind against him. "I want you, boy."

"Mmm" was all he said in response, but he shifted, hooking a leg over my hip so our cocks pressed together as I worked myself against him.

I kissed him hard, thrusting my tongue in and then sucking on his lower lip until he whimpered. I would never get enough of that sound. When the need for air made me pull back, he stared up at me, eyes glazed over. The sight of him so passion-drunk made me groan.

"Daddy," he whispered. "I was a bad boy. I didn't listen to you. I didn't return your calls."

I shook my head. "Avery, I'm the one who—"

He laid a finger over my lips. "I need this." Color rose in his cheeks. "I don't know why, but just play along. Please."

His cheeks were flushed, and I could tell he was nervous about what he wanted to say. "It's okay, boy. Tell me what you need."

He nodded, but he didn't say anything else, so I encouraged him. "You've been a bad boy, and you need Daddy to help you be better?"

He nodded. "Yes, Daddy. I'm sorry. Are you going to spank me?"

His words made my hands itch to slap his gorgeous ass, to make it red and burning hot. "If I do, will that help you remember to be good?"

"Yes, Daddy. Yes, it will."

"Good. Because I am going to spank you. Hard. It's going to hurt. Because that's what bad boys need."

"I do. I need that." I almost laughed, because he sounded so ridiculously eager.

"I can already tell you really want to be good."

He looked up, eyes wide, lips pouty. "I do. I just forgot."

This was going to be so much fun. I dashed into the bathroom for a towel, spread it on the floor at the end of the bed, and sat down on the edge of the mattress, which was low to the ground, as if designed for exactly this. "Come here and lay over my lap."

"D-do you want me to strip first, Daddy?"

I hadn't intended for him to, thinking it might make him feel too vulnerable, but if he was asking…

"Yes, boy. Get naked and then get over here."

Avery's hands shook as he pulled his shirt over his head and tossed it aside. I smiled at him, wanting to show my approval as he toed off his shoes and then pushed his shorts and briefs down his legs.

Completely naked now, he knelt beside me.

"Boy?"

"Y-yes?"

"If you need me to stop, what do you say?"

"Red."

"Good boy."

He shivered as he positioned himself over my legs. I was already hard, but my cock stiffened more as he wiggled around. I wanted to release it, to order him to suck me off, but I didn't. There would be time for that later. This was for Avery.

"It's okay if you need to cry," I told him. "Daddy doesn't mind tears. I want you to let everything out: scream, beg, cry, whatever you need to do."

"Yes, Daddy."

I rubbed my hand over his ass and then squeezed his cheek, digging my fingers in. He sucked in his breath and wriggled.

I smacked him hard and he jumped. "Stay still."

"Yes... Daddy." His breathing was already harsh.

"Brace yourself. I'm not going to go easy on you."

"That's what I need."

I spanked his other cheek then, enough to really sting, but still not with my full power.

He tensed. I could tell how hard he was fighting to keep from working his hips. "Breathe, boy. You have to relax into it, or it will be a lot harder."

"I'll try, Daddy." He sounded so earnest. I wanted to kiss him as much as I wanted to make his ass ache.

I spanked him again and again, sometimes alternating cheeks, sometimes hitting the same spot several times in a row. I held him against me with an arm across his waist, knowing he wasn't going to be able to keep from struggling, no matter how much he wanted to. But eventually, I felt him give. He started arching toward the blows instead of trying to escape. I loved that I could do this to him.

"You're doing so good, boy." I paused and rubbed his ass. "You're taking your punishment so well."

"Thank you, Daddy." His voice sounded choked, and I felt tears wetting my leg. That's what I wanted, for him to let out all his pain and fear.

"I'm going to start again, and it's going to be harder this time. It's okay to cry, boy. Remember that."

He nodded and shifted himself a bit, as if making sure he was braced against the blows. I kissed the reddest part of his ass, loving how hot his skin was. Then I hit him harder than I had before.

CHAPTER FIFTEEN

AVERY

"Daddy!" I cried, so loud I was sure I could be heard down the hall.

He spanked me again, and it hurt so bad, my tears began to fall faster. I squeezed my eyes shut, trying to hold them back, despite what he'd said. Part of me wanted to cry. But for some reason I couldn't let go.

"More. Please." My voice was strangled, the words barely coming out past the lump in my throat.

He gave me the hardest blow yet. It rocked me forward and made me keen. He didn't slow down, spanking me again and again. "Hurts. Jesus, it hurts."

"I know, baby."

Those gentle words were what finally let me release it all. I sobbed as the next blows came. He kept going and the pain shifted. I was still crying, but I was so hard I worked my hips, rubbing my cock against his leg. "I need. I need... so much."

"I know, boy." He laid a hand on the back of my neck, holding me in place. "I'll give you what you need."

More slaps. More pain. My body was singing. I sobbed and begged, and then I was right there, ready to come. "Daddy! Daddy, please. I can't hold back." I bucked against him as I shot on his legs and the towel.

It took me a few moments to realize he was stroking my back and talking to me. "So beautiful, boy. The way you surrendered was incredible."

I turned my head so I could look at him. "Thank you, Graham."

His eyes widened. "You... Wow."

His name. Was that why he looked so shocked, because I'd used his name? "You like that?" My voice was scratchy. Had I been shouting more than I realized?

"I... Yeah. I love it when you call me Daddy, but right now I like you using my name."

I tried to sit back and winced. Damn, my ass was sore, and it was going to be that way for a long time. I didn't mind, though. The main thing I wanted in that moment was to please him like he'd pleased me.

"Daddy?"

"Yes, boy?"

"May I suck your cock now? I want to thank you properly."

He groaned. "Fuck, yes." He couldn't seem to get his pants undone fast enough.

When his cock sprang free, I took it down and sucked it like it was the most delicious thing I'd ever put in my mouth, which really, it was.

At first he didn't touch me. He just worked his hips the little he could while seated on the end of the bed. But eventually, as more precum started to slide down my throat, he took hold of my head. I relaxed and let him take control. He pulled me all the way down until my nose touched his bush. I reveled in having my throat full of him. When he let me go, I sucked in enough air to speak. "Come on my face. Please, Daddy."

He gripped his cock. After only a few pulls, he grunted and came, his seed landing on my lips and cheeks. I opened my mouth, wanting some in me too. When he finished, I swiped my tongue around my lips, cleaning up what I could. Graham licked up the rest.

After a filthy, cum-filled kiss, he looked me over. "Are you okay?"

I nodded. "Yeah. You knew exactly what I needed. I've been spanked before, but never like that. Never enough to make me feel like I was shattering and then coming back together." Tears stung my eyes again. "I'm sorry. I just…" It was all too much. Finding him. Feeling betrayed. Running away, coming back and then what he'd done for me.

"Come here, boy. Let me hold you." He helped me stand. Then we stretched out on the bed with me on my side, cradled against his chest. I smiled as I wondered how long it would be before I could stand to lie on my back.

"What?" Graham asked as my smile widened.

"My ass feels like it's on fire," I said, wiping my tears away.

"And that makes you smile?"

I sniffled and then laughed a bit. "Yeah."

He kissed the top of my head. "Good, because I'd really like to do that again. And maybe…"

"Maybe what?"

"I'll use my belt next time."

"Oh God, yes."

He wrapped his arms around me, and I breathed in his scent. "I love being your boy."

"I'm glad, because I love taking care of you." He put a finger under my chin and tilted my head so I looked up at him. "I'm going to hold you until you feel settled, and then we're going to order dinner, curl up on the couch, and watch *Bridget Jones*."

"And drink Frappuccinos?"

"Hmm. Maybe, but I'll have to bribe someone to bring them to us, because I'm not leaving you until I go back to Charlotte. I want every single minute I have with you."

I sighed. "I want that too."

***

Later, I lay on top of Graham on the couch. The remains of the Frappuccinos I'd convinced Sean to bring us—caramel for him, peppermint mocha for me—sat on the coffee table. Every once in a while Graham's hand would drift down to caress my ass, and I'd sigh because while the rasp of his fingers over the sore skin hurt, I loved the reminder of what we could be for each other. Yes, this was new. Yes it was crazy fast, but we had so much potential.

"Daddy?" I said, hoping he wouldn't care that I was interrupting the Just As You Are speech.

He turned and looked at me. "Yes?"

"I know two weeks isn't all that long."

He groaned. "It's a fucking eternity."

"So I was hoping you'd Skype with me and maybe we could… play some."

"You want me to Skype sex you?"

I nodded. "Skype Daddy sex."

"Boy, that is a fantastic idea."

Relief washed over me. "Okay, and I also wanted to know if I could call if… if I just wanted to talk or share things with you. I know you're busy, but—"

He slid his fingers through my hair, massaging my scalp. "I'm not going to be too busy for you, Avery.

127

If you need me for anything, even if it's just to chat, I want to be there."

I frowned. "But you—"

"Obviously I have meetings I need to attend, just like you have appointments with clients, but I'm not such a workaholic that I won't take time to talk to you. I don't just want a man to have hot sex with. I want to share my life with you."

"Whoa." I was stunned. He really was serious about this.

He winced and turned away. "Maybe that was a bit much."

"No, Graham." I touched his cheek and made him look at me. "It wasn't. The thing is, I feel so much for you. I want all that too."

He smiled then, looking so very happy. "Kiss me, boy."

I did, and it was the sweetest, most love-filled kiss I'd ever had.

Want to know what happens next for Graham and Avery? After the Weekend (Love and Care Book 2) is coming August 2018.

Dear Reader,

Thank you for purchasing *Father of the Groom*. I hope you enjoyed it. If you like age gap romance you may also enjoy the *Thorne and Dash* series which starts with *Professional Distance* as well as *A Chance at Love* which is a stand-alone title. I offer a free book to anyone who joins my mailing list. To learn more, go to silviaviolet.com/newsletter.

Please consider leaving a review where you purchased this ebook or on Goodreads. Reviews and word-of-mouth recommendations are vital to independent authors.

I love hearing from readers. You can chat with me on Facebook in Silvia's Salon, and you can email me at silviaviolet@gmail.com. To read excerpts from all of my titles, visit my website: silviaviolet.com

Silvia Violet

Author Bio

Silvia Violet writes fun, sexy stories that will leave you smiling and satisfied. She has a thing for characters who are in need of comfort and enjoys helping them surrender to love even when they doubt it exists. Silvia's stories include sizzling contemporaries, paranormals, and historicals. When she needs a break from listening to the voices in her head, she spends time baking, taking long walks, curling up with her favorite books, and spending time with her family.

Website: silviaviolet.com

Facebook: facebook.com/silvia.violet

Facebook Group: Silvia's Salon

Twitter: @Silvia_Violet

Instagram: @silvia.violet

Pinterest: pinterest.com/silviaviolet/

Titles by Silvia Violet

Lace-Covered Compromise
A Chance at Love
Coming Clean
If Wishes Were Horses
Revolutionary Temptation
Of Hope and Anguish
Three Under the Christmas Tree
Needing A Little Christmas

Fitting In
Fitting In
Sorting Out
Burning Up
Going Deep
Getting Hitched

Thorne and Dash
Professional Distance
Personal Entanglement
Perfect Alignment
Well Tailored (A Thorne and Dash Companion Story)

Ames Bridge
Down on the Farm
The Past Comes Home
Tied to Home

Unexpected
Unexpected Rescue
Unexpected Trust
Unexpected Engagement

Law and Supernatural Order
Sex on the Hoof
Paws on Me
Dinner at Foxy's
Hoofing' It To The Altar

Wild R Farm
Finding Release
Arresting Love
Embracing Need
Taming Tristan
Willing Hands
Shifting Hearts
Wild R Christmas

36241831R00080

Printed in Poland
by Amazon Fulfillment
Poland Sp. z o.o., Wrocław